Andr

Perfume and Cigarettes

Austin Macauley Publishers™
London • Cambridge • New York • Shariah

This is a work of fiction. Names, characters, businesses, places, events, locales, and incidents are either the products of the author's imagination or used in a fictitious manner. Any resemblance to actual persons, living or dead, or actual events is purely coincidental.

Ordering Information
Quantity sales: Special discounts are available on quantity purchases by corporations, associations, and others. For details, contact the publisher at the address below.

Publisher's Cataloging-in-Publication data
Szenasi, Andreea Veronica
Perfume and Cigarettes

ISBN 9781645756255 (Paperback)
ISBN 9781645756248 (Hardback)
ISBN 9781645756262 (ePub e-book)

Library of Congress Control Number: 2021900454

www.austinmacauley.com/us

First Published (2021)
Austin Macauley Publishers LLC
40 Wall Street, 33rd Floor, Suite 3302
New York, NY 10005
USA

mail-usa@austinmacauley.com
+1 (646) 5125767

First Part

One Has No Name

1

The front door was closed but wouldn't stop spinning. Aaron was strongly holding the bottle which was still cold in his hand. Aaron hurried and pushed the bottle in front to open the door. The clicking sound of glasses was quick. On the ground were the smashed pieces. He looked down and stepped over it, trying not to fall. His sleeve was soaked and he tried folding it up. Aaron turned at the corner and walked until the back alley with the neck of the broken bottle in his hand and then let it go. He felt like choking and kept wiping the sweat from his face and under his nose. Behind the bowling alley, Aaron was searching for his cigarette packet to take out a smoke. He put it close to his face so he could make it stop moving so fast. The taste in Aaron's mouth was changing. A bitter taste was coming up his throat, covering the back of his tongue and quickly taking out the smoke between his lips. Aaron leaned forward and tried breathing through his mouth, both hands on his bent knees. The taste was getting stronger and then he took a long puff from his smoke. He unzipped his jeans but the warm urine was draining down his legs already. The cigarette was slowly smoking by itself.

A high-pitched sound was hurting his ears when his head hit the cold ground. The image was fading slowly. The cigarette broke and Aaron couldn't feel the sickness anymore. His numb half-opened eye was facing the reflection of a traffic light.

It was this poorly lit place she entered, with only some oval warm neon colors above the bar and cold white lights from the window fridge.

It was smelling funny in there and with her bare feet getting stuck to the bar floor she could feel the looks in the shadow turned on her.

She entered, leaving the heavy door slam behind, the sound of it being covered by the loud stereo music and the drunken laughter, bringing one shaking muddy foot in front of the other. Drops of water falling off her soaked hair, the top of her nose and chin. Leaving small round marks after her.

Her look as she checked around, passing the guys from the bar, was lost and empty.

Within her eyes, everything seemed darker and in yellowish light.

The music was breaking up at some point in the night and with a quick look at her hands, she realized the uncontrollable shaking of them. The raindrops of water hitting the windows were hearable between the changing music.

Her presence was easily noticed even since the beginning and couldn't be forgotten having now and then a pair of eyes turned and looking for her. She was trying to control her chills at a four-seat table from the back of the bar with the waitress coming over, offering her already paid drinks; one of the shots from the owner himself.

I am drunk and it looks like I have; it looked like she had nothing better to do there than to peel her red nail polish off.

'I'm soree,' said a fair-haired man at the end of his middle age who managed to sit on just a quarter of the plastic chair.

'Don't wanna bother. No,' he said, shaking his head. He was pressing his left ear on his palm.

She was standing two seats away from him and his sweaty shirt's, combined with a 'brand new car' black teardrop-shaped car odorant and cheap poured beer, smell was coming towards her.

'Ya look col', colder,' he was fighting to find the word. 'Coldi-er, 'ish,' he said looking away.

The man stretched a jean jacket towards her and held it above the table, with an edge touching the table surface and getting soaked in beer. She had both hands on the empty steamed glass with only beer foam left. Her sleepy eyes fixed on the tv screen from the other side of the bar. Her face was beaten by a green neon light coming from a V sign above some large mirrors in where she could see everything behind.

His intersected look started to be impatient.

'I don' wanna botar you.' He shook the jean jacket, still holding it above the table.

'Ya wan' it or not?' he raised his voice without being able to scream. With a fast and strong movement, he dropped the jacket on the table, with the leaked beer splashing his left cheek. 'I don't want to.' He flipped his thick fingers in the air like it would be no point in explaining. 'I have a daughter. How old are ya?' It was like something was dragging him behind. His chin getting pressed in his neck, his eyes opening wide, then he would lay back forward in the chair.

She did not move. She closed her eyes for a moment and opened them back at the sound of some heavy drums coming from the stereo, wildly getting afraid of falling asleep.

The drunk waved his hands again, looking at her like she was an idiot, stupid for all he knew.

'Nah, my daughter,' he murmured something beneath his breath.

She couldn't be less interested. As a matter of fact, she stopped seeing him next to her; she closed her eyes a couple of times now, quickly opening them after. Was like a weak flickering image of the man next to her.

'After the divorce, nah, you don't know. Ya too y'ang. You don't know,' he said. 'You too young,' he repeated.

He stood, grabbing the back of the warmed seat, and walked away in the raising smoke at the vibrations of the moving floor. Leaving behind, with no intention of taking it, the jean jacket filled already with a bitter smell.

He turned back to her but didn't sit.

'I didn't want to be bather ya.' At that point without looking at him, she had the feeling that the guy was looking through her with cross eyes and dark bags under them.

'I didn't want. I don't, ya know?' He waited for an answer. 'Nah.' The fair hair guy with a crooked face turned around throwing his hands in the air as an insulting gesture.

She was following him in the mirrors while he went back to the bar asking for another beer.

She sat quietly at her table, warming up, waiting for the morning light. Above one of the fridges were some fast-changing colors that played in the corner of her eye. It was red, it was yellow, it was green.

How did I get here?

2

Run, run. Come on, faster!

Her foot pressed against the gas pedal, leaning all of her weight against it. Her eyes fell on the rearview mirror of the car. Her scratched elbows touching over the steady steering wheel with her blond hair sticking to her face. The low static of the radio station was on 97.7 frequency. The car window was stuck halfway up and the rain was coming inside, washing her face in cold raindrops.

With the edge of her sleeve, she was cleaning the windshield, nervously leaving circular marks on it, making it more difficult to see ahead. The washed road in front of her was beaten by the fast, strong headlights. The long path was never finishing and she felt trapped in a loop between the high skinny branches beneath the sky. She was lifting herself up by pressing her left foot on the resting pedal and flinging her chest over the steering wheel.

The drops against the racing car were louder and louder as it passed.

Her lips on the inside were black from too much red wine. Often spitting so she could get rid of the sour taste from her mouth. The small round green stone from her loose necklace was rocking on her chest, leaving a tiny bruise behind.

She lowered her eyes and stared at the golden necklace which got caught onto one shirt button. Her left foot jumped over her right until the black tires stopped on the wet road.

Her slim fingers gently covered the green stone. The rain was slowly passing and the radio lost its frequency, numbers violently switching on the dusty screen near her.

The spongy driver seat was heavier and colder. Her white shirt was partially transparent and with the hand on the locker to open the door, she spit the rainwater out of her mouth onto the steering wheel. Slowly leaking off it.

She stepped outside, jumping at her foot touching the cold road and left the car door open.

She had to sit down for a while. Laying there, leaning her back against the front of the car, between the two pale headlights. The road in front of her was shining and she could see the raindrops slowing down.

Bare feet and with her shirt, which had become transparent, she couldn't stop the shaking of her body. Her face was covered on the sides by her washed out blond hair with the color running down her shoulders. She slid, hitting her left arm and forehead. Stayed laying under one headlight with her eyes open, only seeing the spot in front of her before getting up and walking into a bar minutes later.

3

The room was lit by the streetlights from outside and they were sharing the couch that could be turned into a bed, covering themselves with a cheap sheet that was making her dry skin itch.

The room was quiet but the sheets were moving. She got up to roll over and go back to sleep. Didn't realize what the warm moving feeling between her legs was; if she had, in less than 20 minutes, she would have jumped out of the window bathroom, barely wearing some clothes and bare feet, scared by the sound of the starting engine car.

Her eyes got bigger and she was swallowing often while Allan's breathing was getting closer to her chest. His warm and sweaty hand was going up and down between her legs, under the elastic of her underwear, partially uncovering her body. She slowly tightened up her legs and turned on one side away from him. Warm sweat sticking her thighs together. Footsteps were walking the hardwood floor from above while she stood quietly. Allan dragged her leg aside then grabbed her by her hip, towards him, turning her on the back once again. Her legs were in the shape of a 'P'. A car was parking outside not far from the window. Allan's face got uncovered by the headlights. She was looking directly into his big eyes and yellow face. A sweaty warm feeling was all over her legs and she couldn't get rid of it. Squeezing tighter her thigh before getting cold again.

Allan didn't see her watching him. He was looking down at what he was doing and getting closer. The covering sheet flew in an instant across the couch while she hurried to enter the bathroom. Within the tall pink halls, she grabbed the clothes basket which was empty and turned to look through the doorknob. His heavy body was above the desk searching for a smoke. She was standing in the middle of the toilet hearing the jingle of the keys she took from the desk and letting the water run. She got in the tub after pushing the curtain aside and opened the tiny bathroom window. It was too high to reach for going out with her legs first. The water was still running and the sink was filling up. When putting her arm out the window, she hit the keys on the glass and froze. Turned around and looked at the door. There was no movement on the other side and her heart skipped a beat. She put her feet on the edge of the bathtub and pushed herself out.

She put the keys in her mouth, strongly biting them, trying to push herself out and jump at the same time. The water was louder and she slipped after the last jump by losing the edge of the tub and hit her knee and chin against the wall. The pain was running through her face. The sound was echoing and she could not risk losing more time. She caught the edge of the wooden frame window while the water was pouring out of the sink and pushed with her right foot, getting almost out completely this time. The rubbery carpet was still dry. She stood there, halfway out. Her hands went numb but she pulled one more time. She jumped out of the bathroom window while Allan was waiting for her in the kitchen for a smoke. Smelling his wet fingers with the smoke rising above him. One leg over the other and checking the door.

Her sliding shirt against the wall got unbuttoned. Her elbows were bleeding. Her body hit the cold ground, cutting her lower lip. Her heartbeat was in her ears, louder than ever. Her legs were automatically getting up to run around the block and get to Allan's car. The wind was strong when she was running with the sound of the keys jingling still between her lips and unbuttoned white shirt on the narrow valley into the parking lot.

4

She was stirring the cold coffee with the spoon. The sugar melting at the bottom of the cup. The darkness behind her eyes brightened once with the sun rising. Her shirt was stuck to her body and her barely dried hair was making chills run down her neck. The stereo music of the bar was repeating and the one hand mans from over the night left before morning hit. Her shirt unstuck from the seat when getting up, the spot left warm behind and she went to the exit. The door was covered in a soapy dried mark. She walked outside in a controlled sort of way after her legs went numb on the bar's chair. She stopped next to the road shortly because of the morning wind which was hurting her face. She sat on the road, her legs on the ground, keeping her arms close to her, almost embracing herself. Leaned her head back and put her hair behind her ears. In the corner of her eye, she spotted a blurry, familiar car. The one she left behind. Which she left on the road unlocked and with the keys inside. It was getting closer to her.

Allan.

Allan's eyes were fixed on her and he quickly stopped the car across the road, pushing down the hand brake then slamming the door.

She turned her back to him. Chills going down her spine not only because of the cold.

I should have thrown away those fucking keys.

Allan's heavy steps against the road were running to her, he took off his blue sweater and covered her.

'My God, what happened to you? Why you here alone? You just disappeared last night, oh you're freezing!' the questions went on and on for a while.

With a quick movement of her shoulders, the blue sweater hit the ground. She remained silent.

Allan took it back and covered her once again, not realizing that it didn't fall by itself.

'And how did you get here from the car? Hey. Are you listening?' Allan waved his sweaty hand in front of her.

With the same gesture of her shoulders, she lost the sweater.

'What the…' his eyes were running up and down, through the transparent shirt, stick to her body. With her fingers, she made him a sign for a cigarette. She wanted to swear at him but he turned and she smiled. Took the cigarette carefully out of his hand without touching him and looking him in the eyes.

She spat on him right between those confused eyes. Her tired laughing turned into coughs when seeing that her spit had enough time to drain down his face before cleaning it.

'What's the matter with you!' Allan said, jumping up on his feet. He used the bottom of his sleeve to clean himself and he took one step back.

She again made a sign with her fingers that she needed a lighter.

Confused, Allan took out from his pocket a box of matches. She did not move nor catch the little box thrown at her feet and with a slow twist she covered it with her foot. Allan's eyes, without being able to control it, were falling down her legs, making her one more time squeeze her legs together. From his dirty untied shoes up to his short messy curly hair, he had no shame.

'I could not sleep last night. So I went for a ride,' she said, quietly playing with the smoke between her fingers.

His eyes got bigger, already knowing it before she had to say it. He was a couple of steps away from her but she could dance on his heart beats. She dragged the matches with her foot towards her and opened her legs. She lit the cigarette, coughing at the first puff. Got up and wanted to spit in his face again but seeing his reaction trying to avoid it, a dirty forced smile appeared on her face. Passing him, she felt him shaking.

The salty sweat was filling his palms and he almost ran back at his car. He didn't stay to think about it twice and she knew, he was watching her going ahead in the rearview mirror after turning the car.

* *

The sound of a truck engine was much louder than that of a car and Doug right there was singing louder than the radio. She was still in the passenger seat without singing but beating the rhythm with her leg and holding strong with both hands the seat belt. She was looking at the packet of cigarettes on the dashboard but she was too ashamed to ask for one; Doug saw her staring and at the first gas stop, he returned with two packets, one of those were blue Lucky Strike for her.

By the time she opened the packet and put the smoke in her mouth, Doug had already let the windows down for them to smoke. She let her head rest on the back of the seat, closed her eyes feeling the heavy wind running inside. The ash from both cigarettes falling inside the truck at the sound of empty Red Bull cans rolling and the hanged pair of dices by the rearview mirror which was continuously spinning.

'Where ya heading?' he screamed over the cracked window.

'Ahead,' she said, raising her head.

'Lucky you. I'm going the same way. Need a ride?'

She stood from the cut tree trunk she was resting and jumped into the truck.

'Oh, long way you had right there,' he said after she sat and slam the door. 'Doug my name is,' he foolishly said. Doug turned and look around behind the driver seat. His eyebrows raised when he found what he was looking for. 'I've got no shoes in here but here you go,' he handed over a red shirt.

A checkered red shirt was covering the dried transparent shirt she was wearing. Her green necklace still cold on her chest. Doug was always holding an old yellow rag around with which he would wipe his forehead under his cap. They passed a couple of villages on their way but mostly long fields or tight roads with tall slim branches. The sky was getting a uniform grey color, covered by clouds.

‘Wanna crack open another one?’ Doug pointed at the Red Bull cans from under her seat.

Hours passed in the sweat-smelling cabin truck combined with strong put out cigarettes. The sound of another energizer opening one after another and the hand from the speed changing moving in her left sight. The headlights grew stronger on the dark road as the day was passing. Her restless face was uncomfortably moving at the jumping of the truck. Doug put up the window as the air was cooling. Far lights were raising from ahead and soon they would enter the city. She took off her seat belt and buttoned up the red shirt. Held tight the cigarette packet and drink up the can of Red Bull.

‘All the way down.’

She did not move since Doug left her on the road. The horn of the leaving truck was stronger than the repeatedly lighter against the wind. She looked up with the cigarette stuck between her lips, blowing the smoke between the corner of her mouth and following with her eyes the two red spots from the back of the truck. In the open field getting further, the two spots were losing and after a curve, disappearing. The cold air covered her legs and cut her breath at each drag of the cigarette. Her toes were lifted up and she looked down moving them, getting smoke into her eyes. Warm blood leaking from the cracks of her bottom lip and covering half of the cigarette filter. Facing her feet, she put one foot in front of the other, easily pushing the heel and having the rest slide on the freezing road. She was going forward next to the washed out painted white line when at the drop of her cigarette she shut her eyes.

A dark blue colored car, seeming black in the night, was blinding her with its golden headlights. She turned her eyes upon it and kept going. The car was backing up. It was going in the same direction she came from. She passed it at the sound of a slamming door.

'You're all right? Need help? A ride?' the questions were flowing. He was tall and young. Black hair barely touching his shoulders, his hand on her arm. She nodded that there's nothing and continued ahead. The air was changing and it was easier to breathe. The car engine and the grass moving in the wind were surrounding them along with her heavy clumsy steps.

'Look, I can drive you in the city, it's 20 minutes by car. I live not too far from here. You can call someone from there if you want.'

She saw the flickering lights in the distance. Cold drops were touching the top of the head.

'You got a coin?' she asked.

He searched his pocket and stopped.

'I have a phone if you need to call someone. It's better than searching for a phone cabin. You won't find one until you're in the city.'

She said nothing.

'I can wait with you for someone to pick you up.'

'You have a coin?' she repeated.

He took a deep breath and took some coins out of his pocket.

'Here,' he handed them all over.

'We'll need just one. Flip it.'

He put back the rest of them and keep one in his hand.

'Head or tails?' he said, amused, while the raindrops were more frequent.

'I already know. Just flip it.'

Under the grey sky and the strong headlights, he carefully threw the coin in the air and followed it with his eye, catching it.'

'Heads,' Gabriel raised his hand so that she could see. 'I suppose that was your choice, right?'

'And why are you supposing that?'

'Women, in general, tend to choose heads.'

Her toes were constantly moving against the cold road. Somewhere in the field, the trees seemed to be moving. The darkness had fallen and with it, fresh raindrops were covering both of them. Her eyes peacefully closed and her body continued shaking.

'You don't live too far?'

'10 minutes tops,' Gabriel answered.

Gabriel didn't rush into the car and she got in walking by the back of it. Being watched passing and beaten by the flashlights made her feel uncomfortable.

Tails. She thought of telling him what she did choose.

The seatbelt was holding her body. Inside the car, the noise from the raindrops was constant. Outside the window on the sky, there were empty holes where the clouds had moved fast away and left it uncovered. The car was heading in the same direction she came from but took a right turn, on a rocky road. She looked closer outside. She did not see this road before. The path was clear and from her side of the window she could see not so much over the growing field but a sight of the road. Shadows were falling on her sleepy face. Her heartbeat was loud in her ears and she could breathe only through her mouth. Her body was heavy. With an impulse, her eyes got bigger because of the energizing she had before. There were no empty cans rolling into each other in this car but a low static from the radio. Gabriel slowed down. In front, the golden headlights were falling on the loaded porch full with rusty car parts. One could not see a lot in that darkness.

Really less than 10 minutes, she thought.

The rocky stones felt sharp under her feet when she got out of the car. The far lights of the city were no longer there but got lost between the rich branches. Gabriel rushed near the unlocked door and switched the lights on. A weak light which wasn't hurting her eyes was uncovering the whole porch with Gabriel pushing aside a metal chair with a box on it. She was slowly swinging herself without realizing. On each side of the door were two windows with the left one broken at the bottom. Covered by a thin blue curtain. The pieces felt over the junk and some were still holding on the frame. The house inside was covered in a dust layer and footprints were forming behind her step. Her vision got more and more blurry.

5

The bright pale light was over her. Her chest lifting up and down.

It's a vague memory she has. White foam that seems like gelatin was on the surface of the tub's wall and covering her.

Falling asleep in your own vomit.

The chills from the open window were moving the nylon curtain; she did not realize where that sound was coming from. She tried to catch some of the tub water in her palm to drink it. Raising her hand, she saw it covered in a gelatin looking foam which was leaking out of it. With her mouth so dry she couldn't control herself but to drink it.

Her green necklace was floating on the surface above her naked body. She forcefully caught the edge of the bathtub and started to spit until the water was mixing again with her vomit. Her breathing was alike with that of a ticking clock. Her right hand was floating gently on the waving surface of the water and the other was holding the ice wall. Her blue veins were swollen on her pale skin, her eyes bloodshot and her dry lips stuck together. Drops of water fell from the tap into the sink. The vomit from the water surface was slowly waving in circles at her chest moving. Bitter blood dropping from her cracked lips down her chin, sliding her neck. Her short blond hair curled around her ears. The smell of cigarettes was filling the bathroom, from her soaked clothes.

Something was moving in the next room. Heavy steps getting closer, then stopped at the door.

There he was. Gabriel.

The nice guy who picked her up the night before and told her she could take a bath if she felt like. He was in his un-ironed cotton pants, covering his mouth and nose with the sleeve of the shirt. Gabriel lifted his other sleeve, took out the stopper and waited for the water to drain.

His lips were slowly moving without saying a word but his eyeballs were spinning in every direction. He started the warm water, checking it with his hand and got up to rinse off the leftover vomit from inside the tub. She was struggling to keep her head on her shoulders. She was getting sick from the scented coconut soap left behind on her skin by the yellow sponge and Gabriel often stepped back in case she'll vomit again. Beneath her was a towel which was warming up with the water passing over. Gabriel turned off the shower while drops were licking down her face and hair. She lay down on her back in the tub, holding the edges. Turning over on one side she was already seeing herself sleeping in there. Gabriel gently took her out the freezing tub. He wiped the drops of water from her pale skin with a new dried towel he took from a cabinet. Her lost look was meeting his and Gabriel couldn't help but smile. He brought some clothes from another room. A pair of Fila black large pants with a huge T-shirt, so huge that the sleeves were over her elbows. Her butt and hands were still on the edge, her knees bent and close to each other, her back arched and her head lay behind. He was close to her. He stopped and looked at her for a moment. His hands holding the towel on her shoulders. She was staring into his big round eyes, his lips, and eyes again. Blinking faster as his face was getting closer to hers. He kissed her on the nose, turned around to take the clothes from the toilet seat and dressed her up. The towel which was under her in the bathtub together with her cigarette-soaked clothes were in a plastic container with hot water and detergent. She was in Gabriel's arms. Her face close to his neck and her skin touched by his warm breath. Fresh cold air was filling the room because of the opened window. She was at the end, in a warm bed. Gabriel covered her with two blankets and closed the toilet door and the window. She had an odd feeling. Her feet were still cold and the bones from above her shoulders and arm were hurting. Her right cheek was getting a bruise on it but did not hurt her.

'Try and get some rest,' Gabriel whispered.

In a slight way, he was covered with the scent of her vomit but his hands were still smelling like coconut. His sleeves wet and his cotton pants were making a funny sound each time he was moving around. The last thing she saw before falling asleep was him.

The Farmer

'Our love is a lie and so foolishly layin',' Gabriel was repeating the lyrics with his mouth full. Crumbs falling all over the seat from his tomato grilled cheese sandwich. Driving with 40/h at 5 o'clock on a Friday morning.

'Oh no.' One slice of tomato slipped out on his blue uniform pants. 'Shit,' Gabriel said swallowing the food.

'W'erever ya do.'

The sky was losing its darkness. An orange line rose in the horizon. Through the stained and filthy front window it all looked cloudy. The road around that time in the morning was tranquil. Nobody to disturb. No one hurrying.

Gabriel humming the music in his car, holding the grilled cheese in his left hand and driving on the long road ahead of him.

He arrived 20 minutes earlier in the factory parking.

'Hits you when it's too late, too late.', 'too late, too late', 'too late', 'too late, too late'.'

He quickly took out the cd and turned it. It was all scratched on the back.

Well, at least it didn't stop while driving still.

'Gabriel, hello!' One of his coworkers was near the door smoking his Chesterfield cigarette.

Gabriel had the smoke between his fingers and lit it up after closing the car door.

'Morning there,' Gabriel said.

In his mind, he was still humming the song.

'How are ya, young fella?'

Will worked there since the beginning. More years than all of them together. A local known by all. That morning his bags under his eyes were more pronounced than the rest of the days.

'It's getting windy outside, my friend,' Gabriel said. He was smoking and stopped in front of Will. Put his hand in his pocket and looked far at the sky.

'Rains coming though.'

‘Rain?’ Gabriel asked.

‘Waking up with the TV news on, hmmm?’ a former employee said, coming near the sidewalk.

‘Well, well. Look who showed up around,’ Will excitedly said.

‘What you bastards doing?’ he took out some matches from his pocket and lit up his smoke.

‘Same old, same old. You passing by, hmmm, walking today?’ Will asked.

‘Nah, gotta go to the shop today. I left my car over there. I’ll have to fix the fender ’cause it was rusty everywhere.’ He turned his eyes away. ‘You know Gabe, the offer is still on if interested.’

‘I know,’ Gabriel said under his breath.

‘Let me know if you change your mind, any time.’

He nodded.

All three of them took a smoke at the same time in silence.

‘My knee hurts. Will rain today,’ Will said after a while massaging his knee.

A wave of laughter started.

‘You old folks and your joints pain predictions,’ Ryan said, still laughing. He finished his smoke and threw it away.

Gabriel entered the fabric with a buttery stain on his uniform pants from the tomato and his badge moving on his chest. Punched in and went to his workstation.

Square uncut cartoon boards were regularly moving together on the moving band. Gabriel’s job was to cut the boards in little matching pieces with a not-so-difficult machine to use. It will press the carton with the puzzle shaped blades and cut it. On each side, he had to press two buttons simultaneously or it wouldn't cut. One could not forget their hand on the band or end up chopping it off, coloring the moving band. Warm blood leaking down and covering the cartoon in dark red. The next one, another guy will have to put the puzzle in plastic bags, boxes and layer them. The models were changing. There were different sizes, a lot of images, for children above four to five years old with 100 pieces to images of German castles with 1000-1500 pieces. That day was one with over 100. A woman from the image was walking down, and up at the same time. Half of the stairs upside down as well as the people from it. The puzzle was in shapes of beige, brown and yellow colors with a black circle going around it.

'Stayin' alive,' Gabriel pressed the buttons.

The sharp blades cut the cartoon boards in perfect pieces.

'Stayin' alive.'

And press.

'And we're staying alive.'

Press.

The next guy who's putting the pieces into plastic bags has to make sure that there are no pieces stuck together.

'Alive.'

Gabriel pressed. He stayed still, singing and pressing for a couple more hours until lunch time.

He realized the grey sky coming, moving fast from west when getting into the car to go home.

The old folk was right again. Him and his knee.

Gabriel left with no music on. Going the same usual and familiar road, out the city, passing the factory, the train station, a bar.

'What the…' Gabriel stopped right away. He'd seen nothing like that before. A girl in a red shirt smoking on the edge of the road. Moving slowly.

Will start raining pretty soon.

'You got a coin?' she asked.

Home.

6

Wandering on the alley she remembered the train station Gabriel told her about a few days ago. Should be on the right side somewhere. She was taking her time to finish eating her jam toast on the way. The striped brown and yellow sweater she was wearing was just a little bit higher than her knees and the cold was coming in under it. She cut the pair of jeans in the kitchen with a pair of scissors which had dried glue on the handle; she kept rolling them up but they wouldn't stay. Stepping on them without realizing. The sleeves were three times rolled up and even like that they covered her elbows. No longer with bare feet but with a green pair of sneakers one size bigger and an orange T-shirt under. She finished the last bite of toast when leaving the path which was heading out on the road. Leaving on the same road that got her at the farm. Everything has an ending; that's why we end up from where we began. The early morning cold air was waking her up. Not far in the distance before the curve, a couple of lights caught her attention. Passing them she would see a slight and shadowy reflection of herself in a bar window.

Arriving early at the deserted train station, she had to pull up the sock which fell off in her bigger-than-her-foot sneaker. From the beginning, at the farm, she kept fighting the urge of leaving that place. Being out of there, she found herself sliding her eyes on the train lines. She did not bother watching the program telescreen with the hours and destinations nor did she buy a ticket. She walked on the middle of the sidewalk along with the lines. Stopped under a yellow light and looked ahead where the image began clearing up. The first train arrived eight minutes after. On the second line. One, two, three steps, she was inside. Sat down in the sixth wagon next to the window which mostly reflected the whole cabin but her. Above the chairs in the cabin were two vertical mirrors. From outside the color of the train was reddish or maybe brown, she could not say exactly because of the weak light.

She put the black Nike backpack in the chair next to her and tries to sit so she won't feel the cold. The morning light warms her face after a couple of stations. With each passing minute, she gets further from the place she left. The image was moving with the same speed out the window. The worst thing about not having a ticket will be in leaving the train if not paying on the spot. She would leave long before having to.

Back at the farm, she took two bottles of water which she put in the lateral pockets of the backpack. She saw an opened bag with dried out mini croissants, rolled them in napkins, and threw them in a plastic bag. Besides those, she has with her two tangerines, a brown-spotted banana, and a green onion with a sour cream bag of chips. The two shirts she arrived at the farm with were at the bottom of the backpack and a packet of smokes in the sweater pocket with 13 smokes left.

She was getting more and more nervous about how familiar she felt like.

Put her legs down and push herself up with the palms against the edge of the chair with the train still moving. Above her, in the cabin, she saw a black cap on a hanger under the number 22. In the hall with the backpack on her left shoulder, the image outside the window was slowing down. She fixed the cap on her head and light a cigarette in the station. 12.

She would not leave; was like waiting for someone. The familiar feeling was scary for her. She rushed out, almost tripping on her clumsy steps.

Everything has an ending. But no one was coming. She held back her tears and walked away.

Stopped near a small lake when finished smoking. She kneeled down near a fisherman who she did not notice. The golden sunlight reflected on the surface of the lake. Her breath was running out her mouth, the steam like she was still smoking. Her eyes got bigger at the sound of the fisherman who jumped out of the chair. His hands were strongly holding a red fishing rod out of fiberglass, around 2 meters long. He grabbed the hook and pulled it out the back of the fish mouth with one single movement. The sound of the fighting fish beating against the lid of one box disappeared after a while.

She stayed still on the cold and humid ground, breathing in her hands to warm them.

'The amateurs are buying stable fishing rods 'cause they're not feeling comfortable with an elastic one,' the fisherman said. 'Around two hours at 1000°C.' The fisherman continued after a while, looking down on her from his left. 'The skull, the column, the bones of the hip and a big part of the brain are only left behind,' he was describing her, pointing with his finger.

She raised her face.

The fisher was pale but with his forehead in a dark pink burned color with white spots. Dead skin falling off it, his arm joints and elbow. He sat down next to her throwing one leg on top of another after fixing the fishing rod. Light up a smoke while covering it with his palm against the wind.

'They are covered in dust and ash,' he rose, moving his boot. 'Ehhh, it's just cancer, comes out when washed.'

The cigarette smoke was moving in her direction along with the wind and he was telling her stories with huge eyes when talking. Shaking his head again and again.

'I burn people for a living sweetheart,' he said, looking back at his fishing rod. Grey, white spots here and there in his black hair and unshaven chin.

Her hands were warmed up.

'See that unpaved road over there?' the fisher was facing it and she had to turn on her right to see.

He was showing her an old countryside road passing near the lake. Huge trees on one side of it and she raised her head to see further.

'Now then, I planted a young cherry tree a long time ago.' The fisherman was following her with the corner of his eye. 'Hope it will grow old with me,' he giggled.

She looked closer to the fisherman but he covered his face with his left hand as if resting on it. *Cherry?*

'If you take that road, follow it.' He paused to drag a smoke. 'You will end up in front of the salvation, as I like to call it. The old crematory building. We're getting old together. I lose my hair and the layer of paint is falling off. You know sweetheart, some of them out there don't want to go in a box underground and wait for the worms to eat them.' The fisher got up and in front of her eyes, he stepped on the red Lucky Strike cigarette filter.

'What are you gonna do?' she asked at the very end.

Took his stuff without answering and headed to the path.

'I want my body to burn in the same place I burned others and have my ashes thrown in this lake, fed to the fishes,' he yelled with his back turned at her before disappearing between the messy sharp branches.

Looking back, she saw a pair of sunglasses left behind. Pick them up and wanted to shout after the fisherman. Stand and hurry to the path to give back the sunglasses when she found herself searching for it. Bushes and branches all over the place but no path to be seen. Went back from where she was standing before and again, nothing. Took her backpack from the ground and walked away. Took and held her green stone necklace in her hand before hitting the road.

7

The whole day seemed to pass slowly. She fixed her cap and shortly forgot about the fisherman. The air was dry after walking from the lake and the strong afternoon sun was above her head. There was a big green space on her left, a tall fence going around it. An Irish bar on the corner next to a store and some garages not far away. She was eating the leftover mini croissants. She had chocolate on the corner of her mouth and sticky crumbs on the top of her fingers. In the warm weather, she had already emptied one bottle of water. She lit up a cigarette. 11.

Throw the backpack on the ground and with the smoke between her lips straight up her arm, her back, and moved her thigh in both directions. Her body felt like being stuck in some way. The cap slipped on one side and the sunglasses fell off. She picked them up but stayed down smoking and drinking water. A moving shadow was covering her face; looking up, in front of her was a not-so-tall and round guy with a white ironed shirt with short sleeves. His shoes were covered in a slight layer of fresh dust. A tie with oblique grey lines and hurried nod. He stopped with his hands in the pockets and straightened up at the slamming door.

Sweat was leaking from under her cap. She continued smoking.

'Tu est tres belle pour fumer,' Robert said looking down on her.

She put her sunglasses on.

'You're not from around, aren't you?' Robert said after a while.

'Passing by.'

Robert was like walking slowly on the spot. Looking left and right at the passing cars.

'Where to?'

'Away,' she turned to face him. 'How far till I get out this town?'

'Pretty much, I guess. I would say a couple of hours walking. Depends.' His moving shoes were seen in her sunglasses' lenses. Robert's shoes seemed cleaned up with a wet napkin and not waited to dry because of the marks left on them. 'I have to get rid of some flyers and my nephew canceled on me to go to a party out of town,' he took a big breath. 'Damn it, I would have preferred to be at a party somewhere away from here. He told me one of his friends stopped at his house to pick him up. He texted me when he was already halfway there to tell me he's not coming. You know, I have to give damn flyers away now. No one in this place want do some extra work.'

She continued smoking, nodding from time to time.

'If you're interested, I saw you sitting here.'

'How much?' she interrupted him. She was waiting for the question.

'$20. It's almost 5 p.m., was supposed to be here till 7 p.m.'

'$30,' she said, coughing the smoke out.

'Too much.'

'You're also paying your nephew 10 per hour, sir?'

He said nothing.

'Let me tell you how we'll do,' he started to get serious. 'I'll give you $20 and I'm going to order something to eat after you're done.' He was approving himself by shaking his head and raised one eyebrow with a kind of pride in his decision.

'I'll need to rent a room over the night then. What am I doing with your $20?'

'Hmmm. There's a place called The Drunken Rabbit. It's a motel not far from here, 40 minutes away I'll say. Walking up the street. It's a cheap place not gonna lie to you, not too much of a comfort but as you said, you're just passing by.'

She threw away the cigarette from her hand. The smoke was rising in the dry air. They both stayed in silence. Robert was looking over her. She was looking at the cigarette. By the time there was no more smoke, she made up her mind.

'Yes?' a slight kind of relief was around Robert.

His heavy steps rushed inside and told her to wait there. Come back with a tiny cartoon box which he was carrying under his armpit. Put it on the ground and take off the transparent tape from above, cutting through with a pair of keys Robert was holding in his right hand. In the opened box were three rows of flyers. He took half of one and handed it to her. They were of a strong red at the top and losing its color near the bottom. It showed a brand-new grey car in the middle of the flyer, the name of the store written in big caliber letters and two phone numbers at the bottom left.

‘If you give all of this away, come in looking for me,’ Robert said, looking away to the street, then went inside holding the cartoon box in his hands.

She turned and took her backpack, slipped it on her shoulder, and held the flyers with both hands. On the sidewalk she decided to put half of them in the lateral pockets; like that, she could hold them with one hand.

22 minutes on the street and she managed to give away seven flyers. In her hand, the pile looks the same. One of those seven flyers took from her was sticking to an empty mochaccino cup from the next garbage can down the street. Persons who seemed to be taking one but they would pass her by with a smile on their faces. She was leaning against a fence and move her hand at a passing someone. She was looking at each of them and laugh out loud when seeing a funny face. They would take out their phones looking at the time or searching for something without searching and put it back in the pocket after passing her. An uncomfortable pressure started in her heel and the back of her knees. Her shadow moved once with the sun beside her and the sweat seemed to slowly stop. Her left arm was itching from holding it out in the same position. People from inside the building were coming out one after another. A couple of women in their 20s stopped near their cars, talked for less than 5 minutes, and then left as soon as possible. She took initiative, getting bored in standing in one place and moving more near the crosswalk. She was smiling and walking toward the people holding out the flyer from her hand. She would place two flyers on top of another so those will look like one. A couple was coming on that side of the sidewalk. The woman wearing a blue cocktail dress, showing her legs

and her long red hair was covering half her back. Next to her was a gray-haired guy with a pair of sunglasses on his head. First, she holds the two overlay out which were taken by the woman and quickly gave another one to the man. A guy coming in a dark blue shirt and jeans, another who was still wearing his uniform from the restaurant he was working at, both left with no flyers in their hands. A curly blond teen in a black tank top and sweatpants, not sweaty but waiting for the night to start jogging. A woman in a shirt and dark colored coat who worked on the other side of the street, an old couple who got in the car parked not too far from her. The kids were easy because of their curiosity. Took a flyer, holding their parent's hand and giggle when had the piece of paper in their hand. Luckily, there was a bus station on the other side and mostly all passed the street. She was taking advantage of the wave of people coming and trying fast to catch their attention. She saw that if from the first line the people would take the flyer, a couple of them would follow. If not, she wouldn't even try. Soon the buses would stop passing so often as before. The pile of papers got smaller. She was keeping them between two fingers. The last of them, she went and put them on the cars, under the wipers. Walking on the street, an old lady who wanted to talk to someone stopped, took and read the flyer, ask her some questions and gave it back.

'Sorry sir, sir! Yes. Could you please tell me what time is it, please?' she asked a passing man.

'18:45,' he said walking away.

At the second car when taking the flyer, the sound of it ripping caught her attention. She did not realize until that point that the bottom ones were actually stuck together. She stopped to detach those, turned them on one side and another, ripping carefully another one, without breaking it. A clear red spot was all over the flyer. She did not move but look closer. She blinked quickly and then start ripping them again; this time without carrying neither if she was breaking them or not. The top one was covered and under them, the red spot got bigger and bigger.

It's not blood, she thought. *It can't be. Can it?*

She looked closer once again but could not lie to herself. It was blood covering those papers. She took a deep breath and quickly run to the first garbage bin she saw and throw them all away. She then dragged her hands along her jeans as if to clean herself from the dried blood. She looked at the car shop and then long up the road.

He took 'em from the box. Robert did it in front of me. He broke the tape in front of me.

She did not want to go back inside but run to the motel and there she would..., but money. She realized she had none. She dragged her palm again along the jeans, repeated in her mind that she'll ask for the money, and get out of there as soon as possible. Took off her cap and pushed the sunglasses up her head. The lights of the street were not turned on yet but weren't too much left until then. Her body was heavy, her vision got blurry, but she shrugged off the feeling.

The shop was quiet and the slamming of the door echoed the whole building. From another room something, a pen holder, fell on the floor. She made a few steps and stopped. The light was strong inside from the white neon above her.

'Robert?' she asked.

The place was not so big from the inside. Robert showed up from a room on the right. He was red in his cheeks and waved with his hand through his hair.

'Well then, I suppose you done?'

'Yeah, give away all of them,' she said looking at the floor.

'Really? All of them? Damn me, all of them.'

A woman came out of the same office. Her shirt was badly buttoned at the bottom. Her hair was messily caught up and her vest had some odd marks on it.

'Oh, she the girl? Amanda, right?' Miriam asked.

'She's no Amanda,' Robert answered.

They both looked at her in silence. Robert came closer to her and put his arm over her shoulders.

'Come into my office,' Robert's hand was all sticking to her back. She did not look at Robert. He then welcomed her to his office. On his desk, the screen of the computer was as turned towards him as possible, enough so one could not see what was going on over there. Robert's chair was big and black, on the opposite side of the desk were two smaller green and uncomfortable ones for whom may enter his office. She could see no personal items. No photos, no random, or cheap decorations nor a living plant. Robert seemed to be in this business for a long time now. Perhaps too long.

'These days,' Robert said while sitting in his chair, 'being fired or getting retired is so Goddamn easy. Look, just the other day I let go of a new guy who did nothing else but watch porn on his computer and then jerking off in the toilet. Jeff didn't have to throw anything into a box but walk out with both hands in his pocket. I swear I don't get these guys,' he stopped talking. Look at her and then searching for something in his drawer.

'It's a local pizzeria where one of my old college classmates owns the place,' he said holding his tie with one hand. 'Here. You can choose what you like.' Then Robert pushed a menu towards her.

'Anything will do. Nothing with pineapples though.'

He put the order and left her for a while in his office.

She was moving her toes and pushing her heel from one side to another, trying to massage them. The air felt closed in there. The office had no windows but ventilation holes in the ceiling. A store covered in glass but none would open. The ventilation was loud in the tiny space but she felt an uncomfortable presence near her. She turned fast and looked beside her but no one was there. She listened carefully but besides the noise of the plugged computers and the ventilation, was quiet. *Why so quiet?* Got up from her seat and turned at the sound of the door opening. The order arrived.

'Come,' Robert said.

She followed him into the hall which was filled with the warm smell of margarita pizza.

Around the counter, it was Miriam, the chatty woman who did not know the term of personal space, Robert in his short-sleeved shirt and she stopped before arriving at the counter.

The first slice, he gave it to her. Robert's hand was holding out for her and a dumb smile was on his face. She got closer and took the slice in her hands. Miriam was moving her lips left and right, checking her out. Robert did not lose his appetite and he was at his second slice while she was yet on the first half of it

'I saw that too. In the morning when I was making lunch for my boys, but then I heard this,' the woman with glasses said and continued to explain Robert.

'They caught the guy?' he asked.

'How I said, I got distracted. The noise coming from the car.' Miriam got so close to her that she could feel her warm spit next to her corner of the mouth when talking.

'How's your husband doing?' Both Robert and Miriam laughed.

'But aren't you a sweetie? Where are you going? You not from around,' the woman said.

'I don't know yet.' She was trying to step back.

'And how did you get here then?' Miriam also stepped back with her and smiled looking at Robert eating one slice after another.

'By train.'

'By train.' The woman fixed her glasses and almost coughed. 'She's funny too Robert. You know, he told me about the motel. Why don't you invite her over your place, Robert? You have plenty of space,' Miriam insisted.

'I'm not. I guess I don't wanna bother.'

'Oh, but you won't, sweetie,' both quickly replied.

'I… No. But thank you.'

The woman dragged her greasy fingers through her dyed ginger hair.

Robert disappeared for an instant and returned with the money.

She looked down at her hand, holding the money. There were $30 and she slipped them in her backpack pocket.

'You can make more if you want,' Robert said straightening up in front of her. Miriam was still with her fingers in her hair and blow her pizza breath in her ears.

'What? You don't trust us?'

'I better go now.'

'But you didn't finish eating, sweetie. Come on. Stay with us a bit more.'

'I really have to go now,' she said and walk away. Miriam was right behind her and caught her arm.

'Oh come on. Where you hurry at? Didn't you say you have nowhere to go?'

Robert came closer to them and lifted up his sleeves.

She looked over at him and then tried to release her arm from Miriam's fingers but she did grab her stronger.

'You can also spend the night over here,' Robert interfered in the end. 'You'll make even more money and you don't have to stay at any motel, sweetie.' He was now also pulling her hair and sniffing it.

From outside the parking, a KIA car stopped. Miriam looked over and instantly let go of her. Robert stepped back and told her to get lost if she doesn't want more money.

A tall guy in a black leather jacket and jeans came forward to open the door when she slipped right out underneath his arm. She holds tight to her cap and moved as fast as she could. The tall man was confusedly looking after her and then entered the store after losing her sight.

A heavy smell of cigarettes hit her while rushing up the street. The road was still circulated. Even with the night falling she could still feel the heat. The pain from her heels was getting stronger and her left shoulder was feeling funny. The smell made her turn her head. In the shadow of the streetlight was a tired long-faced man with a dirty uniform, destroyed hands and he was laying against the steel door.

The Slaughterhouse

Earlier that day in a room with sandstone tiles, to ease the cleaning after, was one left-handed man wearing his washed-out uniform with numerous dried blood spots which turned yellow after too many washes. He was starting the day with a cigarette. His eyes over the year became cold.

He spits turning back his head on the nylon foil he put on the tiles without arranging it.

He hit the animal so hard with a strong shock in the forehead area, giving him a cerebral concussion. Making sure to shut down the central nervous system which directs the sensation of physical pain. Leaving the animal with no instinct of defense.

After the animal stopped fighting, he was stretching for the knife set with steady handles and slightly steamed blade after disinfection and hold it well in his left hand. He was carefully cutting the animal's throat, the jugular vein along with other large veins, avoiding cutting the esophagus and trachea.

He pulled the knife through a single quick movement, splashing the nylon foil with warm blood.

In less than 5 minutes, the animal lost all his blood, flowing into the blood pit.

He cut the abdominal wall from the pubis to the sternum and detached the large intestine from the rectum. Pulled out the entire gastrointestinal tract out of the casing. In the end, he found his joy in cutting out the tongue and tail and taking out the kidneys.

All of the meat will be marked and sold to supermarkets or in smaller quantities to restaurants where it's cooked and placed identically on some plates to be served.

His grandfather told him when he was smaller that the ear of the animal was a symbol to the barbarian victory in which the toreador defeats the bull without mercy. The toreador getting after the bull's ears which he serves it with fresh bread and dried red wine.

He wiped his hands in a yellow cloth cut from some material a few days ago, leaving the marks of his bloody fingers on it.

He was outside the slaughterhouse at the end of the day, leaning against the wall, having a smoke.

From a nearby pillar was a pale light beating him, his shadow behind him, smoking out of his unwashed sticky hands with dirt and dried blood under his nails.

With the filter between his cracked lips, a passing girl with a black cap caught his attention.

8

The motel sign was big enough to be seen from one block away. The red light from it was covering the street. The traffic light from the intersection stopped changing when she passed under it. The walls of the reception were beige. She had a feeling that they were white in the beginning but slowly changed color over the years. A mustard yellow color sofa with a rough material which will make one's skin rash within 5 minutes. It smelled like naphthalene. As she walked in, there was a round wooden table with both chairs covered by two thin blue flat pillows. Behind the reception, the numbered keys seemed like they were thrown away in a bow together with a pair of scissors and some paper towels. Rags also were thrown away here and there over the place. One on the wooden table, one under the sofa and a bunch, soaked in water mixed with Javel, on the counter. A too big picture above the table. The image was creped and not glued properly behind the plastic frame. Showing a pelican on a hook with his head raised. Ash and dust. A turned chess board with round black and brown pieces and dices showing 1 and 1.

From the table, an old man got up and walked to her. He was wearing a white undershirt showing his grey hair chest.

Large jeans with small holes in them. The woman sitting with him was dressed in a red dress which lost its color a long time ago and a plastic bracelet playing on her wrist. Her hair was dark colored with burned ends. Pink cheeks and non-uniformly applied brown lipstick.

'Yes, darling? Wanna use the toilet?' he smiled uncovering his teeth with leftover food gathered on the edges.

'Hmmm, I need a room.' She was looking at the red-dressed woman who got a sensual, at least she was trying to, smile on her face. 'How much for the cheapest one, old man?'

His chin went down hearing old man and both of them started to laugh heavily.

'Ya know,' he put his arm over the counter, 'I like you already. For how long you'll need it darling?' the old man asked.

'Few hours, I'm gone by morning,' she said still looking at the woman.

The old man went behind the counter and searched in the box for a key.

'We don't rent per hour. The less is per night,' he said turning his back to her looking for something in one drawer.

She was looking for a clock around the reception but nothing. The old man got a key and held it on the edge of his fingers in a manner that she could see it. Stuck to the key was a green scotch tape with the number 12 written on it.

'How much ya got there?'

She reached her pockets looking in his eyes and got out $20 and showed it to him. The old man looked at the red-dressed woman and back to her. His lips got tighter and brought his hand at the back of his neck.

'Tell you what. For ya,' he paused, checking her standing still with the money in her hand, 'I'll leave it cheaper.' He was holding the key for the money. 'Hey!' he screamed after her before closing the door. 'Be a good sweetheart and bring the key back in the morning, would ya? Don't make me come for you.'

She let the door close behind her. On the bottom of her backpack somewhere were lying another $10. She walked all the way to the left, passing the doors. In the end, the last door had the number 8 on it. She had to go back and go upstairs. In some of the rooms the lights were turned on but mostly it was quiet. 12. Arriving there, she put the key in the lock and turned looking at the golden number. The door made an awful sound while she pushed it to open with the edge of her sneaker. The smell hit her in the very first second. Between the missing plastic lines of the louver, the red light from the motel sign was warming the room. On her right was a green lamp which was turned on. Slammed the door with her foot and put the backpack on one chair near the bed. She stayed with the clothes on and went to the bathroom which was a mess too. The dirt between the tile spaces seemed moving, a transparent shower curtain splashed all over and the soap was covered in small curly hair. The toilet seat was down, on it a roll of toilet paper. She couldn't see anything in the mirror. Was a blurry image staring at her? She put water in her hands, her sweater sleeves getting wet and cold and tried to clean it. It was a waste of time. She then threw cold water on her face and let it leak off her chin at the sound of the tap closing. Went back to light up a cigarette. 10. It got wet at the filter because of her wet hands. Opened the window and stayed looking out from the bed. The parking lot was empty. *Small city*, she thought. Sitting on the bed, she let the ash fall on the sheets, her sneakers, and carpet. Up the stairs were a pair of heels rushing. Outside the window, a car that seemed like Robert's stopped in the parking lot. She ran back to turn off the lamp. Then hurried back near the window. She dropped her smoke when the door wide opened. A thin silhouette was standing, beating with her heel on the floor. She couldn't see her face. The shadow was falling over her but she did see the long fake leather boots with large heels she heard coming up the stairs. Soft black curly hair touching her shoulders. She was wearing a mini shirt which was too tight for her, no bra, and a striped leopard jacket.

The Hooker

I was sweating and my hair was dragged back by a tattooed hand. Half my face was covered by my black curly hair. He was pulling it more and more and my neck was hurting. His breath was closer to me. He was biting and licking my shoulders, neck and spit next to my ear. Strongly choking me and pushing me over the desk.

I remember hurting my chest so damn hard that I had a blue bruise on it the next day.

He was shouting to me to moan and I had to.

'Moan, my baby doll, harder. You can scream.' His nails hurting me. 'Let it out, let it.'

After all those years I can still hear his hoarse interrupted voice whispering that into my ear.

'You like it, don't you, hm?' Then he would turn violent. 'Fucking doll, spread your legs!' He used to push his fingers down my throat while he would be above me. Smashing my tiny body with his huge weight. Lifting and pushing me how he wanted. Used to tell him it was hurting but just gave him more pleasure. Pushing my legs harder.

When doing anal I knew it will soon be done. I had to lay there moaning hard pleasing him for a little bit longer.

Ending up so sweaty, when he was dragging me over by the hair on the narrow hall to the mattress, that used to be ice cold.

My head was falling down off it. He would not hit my face. Not a bruise on it. The rest of my body was hurting and changing colors of purple and yellow shades spots all the time.

In two years after that afternoon, my period was to come for the first time. As a child, I was always skinny.

I was bleeding for eight days and in a lot of pain. He did not care. He has done me then too, making me suck the top of his fingers with my own blood on them.

He returned in one week, holding a gift for me. It was wrapped in a used cartoon bag from one of his beer cans. It was this red cheap lipstick he bought. I had to untie my ponytail and to take off my shirt. My boobs were getting a form at that time.

I was against the wall and he was pushing his tongue into my mouth.

'Open it doll. Wider.'

He bends me over and carefully apply the cheap red lipstick.

Put me to deepthroat his bad smelling cock.

'Swallow.' It was not enough for him just to taste him nor having it draining off from all over my face to my knees. His dick had a different shape of red on it. He used my white underwear to wipe the lipstick off my lips.

The first time I enjoyed it, I got rid of him right away after.

My boobs were heavier and rounder then and he did not touch me for over two weeks and three days. He came home smelling like alcohol and lay down on the sofa. He was trying to follow the game or something.

With my school uniform still on, I unbuttoned my white shirt all the way down so that my chest will come out nicely and take down my panties.

I put the lipstick without looking into a mirror; he brought me the same one all the time.

I was making my way into the kitchen to take a glass of water when he saw me. He scratched his big balls and came after me.

The glass was half empty when he grabbed my hip. He was licking my face and body, moving his palm all over me. He was inside me before I was able to realize it. His breath was awful so I tried not to face him but he continued kissing me. Both of us were moaning for the first time so hard of pleasure.

'Ahhh.' I enjoyed it. 'Harder, harder.'

He was going so hard and deep that I wasn't able to control my legs' shaking. I was moving my tongue all over his neck and into his mouth, sucking his dried tongue.

'Ahhh.' I was so wet that it was leaking down my legs when he finished inside of me. I pulled his hair, licked him with all my tongue on his unshaved chin, took a not-so-sharp knife from over the shelf above me, kept his head behind and cut as deep and straight his fucking throat as possible as I could have done it.

I don't remember how many times I passed that blade over and over until he stopped spasming nor splashing his salted blood over my horny body.

I kissed my brother on his opened mouth for the last time, the sound of his head crashing on the edge of the table was loud.

'Ah, ah, ah.' My body was covered in his warm blood and I was laying there still tasting him, masturbating, pushing my fingers deep into me so I would cum. I cut my leg by mistake when dropping the knife but didn't stop. I wasn't moaning anymore I can tell; I was almost screaming. My other hand after dropping the knife was above my head holding the corner of the table. My body was arching and it couldn't stop moving and, 'Ahhhhh, oh my fucking god.'

* *

Near the edge of the door, the two of them stood still with the same tiredness in their eyes at the flickering bathroom neon light. The red spot from the carpet caught her attention and quickly took up the cigarette. She went closer to push the door when she jumped at the sound of Liz's palm slamming against it.

She looked down on her. From her cheap boots up her slim fingers.

'Want money just for coming till here or what?' she said.

Liz was smiling hearing the question but felt no shame.

‘Need a lighter,’ she said playing with the red filter cigarette.

The awful sound of the door opening was echoing the room once again and down the hall, the sharp heels were stepping inside. She looked on the bed and took the lighter near the packet and hand it to Liz which after lighting up her cigarette walked to the bathroom. She took the ashtray with her and lay in the corner. Light up another. 9.

Followed Liz wandering around and then finally sat in front of her on the bed. Her purple underwear was showing. They were almost blowing the smoke into each other’s face. Liz was charmingly looking at her the whole time.

‘You didn’t have to,’ Liz started.

‘The car!’ She remembered running to the window. The necklace beating against her chest.

Got up, ran over the ashtray, and went back at the window. Confused, Liz stopped behind her and looked outside.

‘What car you talking about?’

It was gone and that made her feel worse that she didn’t see where it went.

‘It was. Never mind,’ she said shaking her head.

Liz giggled and went closer to her.

‘Haven’t you, by mistake, let’s say meet with Mr. Robert, have you?’ Liz asked.

Her eyes got bigger looking at Liz and wanted to start talking.

‘He’s a sick fella,’ Liz continued. ‘I suggest you stay away from him and his manipulative puppet.’ Liz stopped and curiously looked at her. ‘Say. What does he have on you?’

'Has nothing,' she hurried to reply. 'Talked to him a couple of hours ago.'

'Hmmm. Well, don't. You have no business with a man like that.' Liz went back to lay on the bed and soon fell asleep. She opened the window to throw away the smoke and kneeled down under it.

It was half-past 2 at the moment but she did not know that. She opened her eyes, shadowy seeing everything at first. She was stuck in between the wall and the nightstand. Her joints and knees hurt and she did not try to move yet. She fell asleep again.

She woke up minutes after because of the dryness in her mouth.

Stretched easily to touch her backpack and drag it close to her. Her legs fell forward once with the sound of her left hand hitting the floor. The sound of the plastic bottle while she drank it all with her heavy breathing between the swallowing woke up Liz. She was on her back on the bed with her legs touching the floor. Liz got up and stayed on the edge of the bed, easily swaying to the left and right. Liz took off her leopard jacket and threw herself back on the bed with both hands on her stomach. After leaving the bottle on the floor, she walked to the bathroom.

Liz followed her not long after. She started to put toilet paper on the seat while Liz was drinking cold water from the sink. She did not flash the water nor took off the toilet paper from the seat after her. Liz turned the tap and went back into the room. Hearing her hit the bed.

The cold water woke her up. In the mirror was still a shadowy figure. She wiped the drops with the sleeve and roll them up after. She saw an almost smoked cigarette on top of the table and lit it up in the heated motel room. Took out the bag of chips and leave it on the nightstand next to Liz.

'Until when you have the room darling?' Liz said not turning around.

'Morning. Noon. Till the old dude comes for you,' she said turning on the lamplight. Liz fell asleep on the uncomfortable stable bed in a funny position, almost on her belly with her hands spread wide open. She dropped the key on the floor before closing the door. The dull lighter from the back pocket was moving in her jeans while she was going down the stairs. The filter of the smoke slipped from her numb fingers in the parking lot. She took a quick look at the reception where the music seemed louder and there were two more people around the wooden table. She preferred wandering on the streets than having to go back to that reception.

The sunrise was still far from rising and out of the room, the heat was bearable. She continued walking up the street in the same direction. The streetlights were left behind and before her very eyes was a long way. Her entire body was getting heavier and more tired at every step. The cold water she splashed on her face lost its effect. Not far from her she spotted a gas station. She did not cheek around nor look inside of it but went to the toilet. The sound of the ice refrigerator was louder in the night. Next to it, on the ground, she saw a brick, lifted and took it with her in case the door wouldn't lock from the inside. Her strength left her and instead, she laid down. Covered the brick with her backpack and put her head over it. Almost falling asleep if there wasn't the light bulb hanging above her. The wires uncovered, hanging there steady with no wind in the hot night. She got up leaning against the wall and catch the handle of the door which easily opened. Did not take her too much to find the switch but the light did not turn on. One of the cabins was missing a toilet seat and the second was all burned with cigarette marks. Under the sink was a broken bucket with some old newspapers and pieces of plastic in it. The place seemed to build downhill. She was searching for another light switch but was none around. The leaves began moving violently on the branches. She put her sleeves down and keep going. The thought of getting further and further was keeping her going forward. Took out a cigarette keeping it in the flame enough so it will light itself up. 8. The next curve was going uphill. She took the white shirt over her sweater and continued walking looking at her feet. She was cold but sweating. Her clothes were getting stuck to her back and chest. Her lips cracking more and more. She was walking on the white line on the edge of the road. Walked with quicker steps, sometimes looking at the mist near the road.

From up there, she saw a narrow long street. The houses were on each side of the road, some cars in front of them, a bus station which goes into the city and a church in the middle. Her bottle of water was almost empty. She stopped to open it with her cold hands. The streetlights were close to being turned out.

In front of her, a metal fence around the church made her stop. The church fence was not hard to jump. Holding the bottle of water, she took another zip to wash the cigarette taste and got to jump when sliding her foot. The door simply opened. A long unpaved path was on the middle, from the fence until the door. The mist was getting stronger between the massive tree roots. The air was easy to breathe but hurt her throat because of the cold water she just drank. Turning around she saw that the streetlights turned off. She looked behind again at the wooden door of the church. Minutes passed but then she could see clearly shapes and colors again with the darkness passing.

All the trees were on her right side. With the cold blue sky and the mist, she ran inside. Strongly pulled the wooden door and open it. It was twice as high as her. Above the altar on the wall behind it was a wooden painting with a nun holding white roses. The walls were all in a light green color and the lateral pillars were painted in a strange floral pattern. Round vitrals with one window missing and covered in plastic nylon which will keep her awake. The picture from the frames representing the crosswalk. The long wooden benches from both sides were separated by a golden carpet. While walking to the front, on her left, was a statue of a monk holding a long white lily and a child. On her right was the statue of Madonna in a blue dress and her hands together in prayer.

In the fourth bench on the left side, she laid on the floor and took one small pillow they used to put under their knees when praying and placed it under her head. Then stuck her back next to the bench.

She was in an uncomfortable position but did not have the energy to move again, and the noise from the moving nylon covering the window was making her restless.

She opened her eyes with two layers of dark circles under her eyes and saw the little pillow in front of her. Her forehead was almost touching the other bench. The noise from the nylon stopped.

'You awake, my child?'

Her eyes were wide open.

She moved her eyeballs but couldn't see anyone. Was too afraid looking up when something touched her leg.

She got up and jumped behind.

'Sorry. I'm so sorry. I didn't mean to scare you,' she said gesticulating a lot with her hands. 'I am sorry. I found you here this morning,' she kindly explained. 'Are you all right?'

She stayed on her back and tried to calm down. At the end of the bench, a nun has kneeled near her. Her white dress lighting her pale face.

The nun was smiling but she couldn't look into her eyes. She got up, holding a prayer book in her hands close to her chest and went in front to the altar.

She got up to stay on the bench after a while out of curiosity. Remained silent and watched her the whole time when she was praying. Suddenly turned and look at the painting above the altar when the nun closed the book. She was next to her side in no second and put the prayer book on the bench just in front of her.

'Take your time,' she said.

While she was staring at the book, the nun went to a chamber, left the altar.

The White Dressed Nun

I couldn't open my mouth from the dryness.

Water, now.

My fucking left shoulder was hurting like shit 'cause of that bloody couch.

Right away I threw away the blanket I covered myself with the night, actually couple of hours before. It was covered in dust and stains.

I saw no bottle of water around the bed, in the bed, anywhere in the room.

Opening the door, God, it made a lot of noise. On one of the steps was a 2L beer bottle with some left over in it.

I had to sit down to lift the fucking bottle without falling.

I feel the things around me spinning faster if I closed my eyes.

The taste I've got in my mouth after drinking that warmed up beer wasn't better. That shitty alcohol dries you out faster. I didn't close back the bottle and just left it over there. Didn't care about the moron who's gonna have to clean away all the vomit from the path. Oh my, there was some at every two to four steps from each other. Different by the size, color, and the smell. One of it, the one I was passing by, was kinda transparent with some pieces of, I dunno, pieces of food. The other one reddish, I think that guy wasn't too good with the red wine though.

Arriving at the door, I suddenly remembered by seeing the door press covered in vomit that that was mine. That was my spot last night. My vomit was white liquid, but it smelled.

I pushed it away with one leg from the entrance.

On my right, being already in the hall, the way was blocked by two tables. With a mirror facing two small and differently colored chairs where I was smoking the night before. Going to the left side I entered the messed-up kitchen. Full of empty and opened bottles and between the furniture I spot a pair of green shoes and something broken in the sink. A burned T-shirt and missing chairs. Some pockets of cigarette on the table but none mine.

I opened them, searching for a smoke. The first one, blue Lucky Strike, empty. Second, red Marlboro, didn't like those. The last one has just a lighter inside of it. I took one from the second packet and light it up in the middle of the kitchen. I threw the black lighter on the table and went looking in the first room which had the door open. The windows inside were covered so I barely saw something. I knew there were a couple of people sleeping in there. I saw them laying around. One guy tried to be comfortable on a chair, two others hugging in a bed near the corner and another fat one smashing two passed out guys under him. Sitting there smoking, I felt my mouth going dry again. With every hit that I took, my whole left row of teeth hurt more.

I finally saw a bottle of water on the edge of the bed. Taking it was so easy. Was empty. Fuck.

Some blond girl was saying something while I went back to the kitchen and some of the ash from my cigarette fall on the floor.

In front of the sink, I let the cold water run. I dropped the cigarette on the floor to drink water right out of my dirty hand. Spitting it in in the end on some broken stuff inside the sink. Out again I tried not stepping in any kind of vomit and get out of there. The door of the street was locked.

I couldn't jump the fence 'cause I've got nothing to put my foot on. Going back inside for the key, I saw my reflection into a window. I didn't realize till that point that my tank top was all ripped off on one side and my bigger-sized red bra was showing. In the room, I saw the girl.

'I need you to open the door,' I said that while almost blowing the smoke in her face.

'The fuck do you want?' she sounded angry.

'The key, from the door outside. I gotta go.'

'What the? Don't fucking smoke in here.'

'Then come and open the fucking door so I can fucking leave then,' I whispered loudly.

'Get the hell out of here!'

'Then come and open the door!' I stopped whispering at that point.

'Get out!' And she rolled on the other side to keep sleeping.

I blew the smoke as close to them as I could. The filter, threw it on the carpet near her mattress, looking at her I stepped on it and walked out.

I took a wooden seat with me and the packet of cigarettes from the table but not having any pockets to my pants I put it between my teeth and tried not touching it with my tongue until I jumped the fence. I was smashing the chair on the path, not even trying to avoid the vomit. It was all draining off the wooden legs of the chair.

With the packet still in my mouth, I put one of my legs on the chair and place the other on the door handle to climb it.

I let go of the packet to fall down and a passing man has stopped seeing me like that. Helping me anyway to jump that shit, I bend over, after being on the sidewalk, to pick up and light up another smoke.

My mouth was getting dry again.

'Thank you, sir.'

9

The nun was taking off the two candles from each edge of the altar, the vase with flowers and over the white tablecloth was putting the new purple one. The two lateral tables, she covered those completely and put new candles of the same color. She took out the dried flowers and went back into the chamber.

The pain from her legs suddenly came over her when standing up from her warmed bench. The white dressed nun came out holding a bouquet of roses.

'Yes, how can I.'

'Can I help you?' she said.

'Oh my, I don't…'

She was looking down at the drees covering the nun's shoes. Her bags under the eyes were darker with her face lowered. Her left cheek covered by a blue bruise and blood between her cracked lips.

'Here, take this. Put the roses in the big vase. The smallest of them in the two ones over there,' the nun pointed.

At the entrance of the chamber, the nun put down a bottle for her to water the flowers after. She found herself looking behind at the wooden door. She was looking with the corner of her eye at the bench where her stuff was still on the floor.

'This one doesn't need ironing. Don't you think so?' the nun asked and gave her the robe to put it on the hanger.

'I have to put the purple ones in the front of the wardrobe?' she asked.

'Yes, my child. And let the one with the golden cross outside too.'

Her feet cold as ever, her hands were sometimes shaking and she was helping the white dressed nun to fold and iron the robes for the next day's service.

From inside the chamber, the nylon foil was moving again. She jumped, dropping the robe from her hand when a heavy branch felt outside. A honk of a car hurt her ears and warm sweat was running down her face. Her feet got soaked and ice cold. She hurried out the chamber when a warm hand grabbed her forearm.

'Say, child, what do you know about advent?'

The nylon foil seemed to stop suddenly. Her body shook no more and her sweat was not running down her body.

'I, I don't know. I am not really religious. I don't think I am, was,' she felt strange saying that. Seemed familiar for her, as if she had that conversation before.

'We're starting the decorations from now. In two weeks on the 1st of December, the priest will be lighting the first candle. Christ's second coming at the end of time they say.'

She heard some tires of a car breaking and she went to the window to take a look. The nun appeared next to her, put her arm on her shoulder and turn her around.

'You have nothing to see there, child.'

‘But the sound.’ She pointed out the window. She looked close to the nun’s face who was getting further and then she realized. ‘You said December.’ She paused. ‘How can that be in two weeks from now? We’re in July.’

The nylon foil was making so much noise that she had to cover her ears. She pressed her palms against them. Turned, when a vase close to her broke into pieces and she was facing outside the window to see that there was no wind at all.

The nun dragged her right hand up her knees. Slowly bringing it up between her legs. The dress was caught in the middle. Turning into what it seemed like to be a pair of pants. Getting a closer look, she saw that the color was changing into a deep familiar blue. She wanted to get closer but she hesitated. She forced her eyes shut. Under the pants, a mild fog was coming out. Filling quickly the room before her eyes. The window shook in a thunder rhythm that made her jump ahead. Behind the nun, in the middle of the altar, a long steel pole was lifting up covering her entire face into a sickening yellow shadow. The place was dark. The golden sunlight from outside was not getting inside. Around her chin some white dried skin began falling. Lifting her hand, she could see some red spots here and there. Looked close when the floor turned to dirt. She saw her hands getting thicker. Her blond hair stick to her forehead was losing its washed-out color and curled up into a dark brown. Her watery eyes were hurting. Her feet suddenly fit in the bigger sized sneakers. The nun’s eyes were glistening in the green color of the tiny necklace stone.

The hollow alley was before her eyes. Fall over. The light was green. Was yellow. Now was red.

The golden sunlight was running through the tree branches and the leaves seemed still. The papers from the desk all flew away. The ironed robs falling off the hanger. The nun's eyes were staring close into hers.

'You ask way too many questions,' the white dressed nun whispered, breathing into her mouth.

* *

She found herself peeling apples in the kitchen. The house next door was where the nun lived and took care of. A two-floor poor house with a huge kitchen and two rooms upstairs. A small pink bathroom with a shower in it, something downstairs as a praying corner and an old wooden fence between the garden and the church.

'Oh, he's here. I have to show him the window and I'll be back,' the nun said looking at her.

Seeing the church again she stopped peeling the apple. Something must have happened. Wasn't wind inside the…

And there he was, clumsy Stanley boy. Coming to repair the broken window. Walking side by side with the white dressed nun. Both of them staring at her at the same time. She lowered her look and continued peeling. Dropped the apple and took another.

Walking up the alley in his green cotton pants, an un-ironed shirt with yellow stains under his armpits and messy red hair.

The Stanley

I'm Stanley, and my height, weight, or age does not matter.

I'm in the kitchen taking off my underwear and throw 'em in the sink near me. I'm holding a slice of bread on a metal spatula above the fire of the smallest eye.

The water for my tea starts boiling in the pot and with the water running out of it, I turn the slice on the other side. I pour a half a spoon of honey into the pot while I'm scratching my balls and my feet are sticking to the kitchen floor. Closing the jar, I see the honey draining down on it and I'm passing my hands through it and I lick them both after.

Is getting darker outside after a couple of hours. I was walking around for a while with a glass in my hands hearing the ice cubes moving.

In the corner of the room, I was waiting for the Cerne Relief to dry out before applying the color on the vitrail. Around the glass, I have my supplies, lits, and molds. On the table and beneath were glass fragments, I used to have a carpet over there and my feet were always stepping on them, which I will have to clean after. The ice cubes were the only thing making some noise around this room. The bathroom door was opened and so was the light. I had enough copper foil to finish maybe more than half of the vitrail and I'd have to buy more alcohol for degreasing the surface which has to be painted also.

I was moving around barefoot with the glass in my hand refilling it now and then and the sound of ice cubes following my every step.

* *

The room the nun brought her to was covered in old carpets and opened boxes. Across the window were an uncovered mattress and a wooden cross above it. A bench covered with a handmade blanket and a pair of leather brown boots under it. Another small round green carpet covering the other and tree pair of folded jeans out of the box. Near a tarot packet was a pair of black, snake model heels which she will be wearing before sunrise.

The majority of boxes were filled up with sweaters and shirts in all shapes and colors. The white dressed nun was unpacking some of them and showing them to her. One yellow checkered shirt, which she liked but it had all the neck eaten, a black turtleneck sweater, and a navy-blue shirt. A long autumn black coat, a pair of shiny shoes, and a black hat.

She was looking around and saw some polo T-shirts, an aviator hat, a pair of children shoes and on the edge of the window a strange collection of plastic plane model toys.

She went closer and took one plane in her hand. On the lateral wings of it, the white straight line was covered in blue from a used pen. She could see herself in a train station, the same strong feeling she felt at the station hit her again. She looked behind her and she knew this time that she had to wait for someone. Still, couldn't remember who she had to wait for.

'Father,' the nun said.

'What have you said?' she fearlessly said.

'Further, child,' the nun smiled, taking her by the arm. 'From the window. Now, you don't want to lose your time with some old toys, do you?' Took the toy from her hand. 'Come. I have to show you some nice clothes.' Near to the bench, she covered up a couple of used blue uniforms as if she was hiding them.

10

The room was the same. Opened boxes with finger marks on them from the removed dust. She woke up with the moonlight on her face, beating at her window and on the wooden cross above her bed. A small green spot shining on her chest.

The shadow of the plane toys in the window was falling down the wall, mixing in with the shadow of a skinny branch outside.

She was covered, by the closed smell material blanket until her neck. The white dressed nun had to shake it before leaving it to her.

The room was quiet all night long and seemed to her as if she did not sleep in ages. She could still feel her cold feet under the blanket.

She couldn't remember whether the room was above the kitchen or the praying corner so she moved quietly on her toes in the dark searching for the clothes she got from the box.

She put on the blue polo shirt and the jeans. Looked in her backpack for the oversized sweater and then over it the white shirt. Took the black snaked model heels in her hand, tied the green sneakers to the back of the backpack, and slowly opened the door which did not make a sound. On the narrow stairs, she was pressing her slim fingers against the wall. Her sneakers moving gently, hitting the back of her legs. A cold breeze was suddenly hurting her face and tears of joy were running down her cheek. Her hand lay stronger against the wall but she knew she couldn't lose time. She controlled her tears and continued down the stairs. Her heart jumped when touching the edge of a frame and the painting almost fall if not slamming with the hand holding the heels against it. She could see clearly in the darkness by then and she did not hesitate in running to the door. Not closing it properly behind her but didn't stop for it.

The street was quiet and a warm wave hit her while walking up. It got stronger and she felt the urge to run along the road when she let go of the backpack from her shoulders hoping that the feeling will stop. She took out the packet of cigarettes and threw the lighter inside it.

There she was, walking quickly, echoing the empty street with the sound of her heels. Before the end of the road, she will walk down a path from where she will come out with bloody feet.

The sunrise was less than an hour away and the sky was slowly lighting up. Her clumsy steps sounded far away on the narrow road. Getting closer, running and heavy breathing. She burned the sweater sleeve when lightning the smoke. 7. Looking over her shoulder, she saw a thin path going down between some bushes. Her blurry shadow was falling down in front of her, holding a red spot of a cigarette in her hand and freezing at her feet. Soon getting off the road.

The path was high, the ground dry and full with the outstanding tree roots. She was moving forward holding strongly the filter between her lips and pushing away the many skinny branches with the palm of her hand. Her shirt got covered in dust and spider webs while her sweater sleeves were stuck all the time in thorns. She put down the heels to roll up her jeans. She slid, falling over her cigarette pack. Breaking them. Controlled herself not to scream but inhaled the rising dust in her open mouth. Smashed the packet and got her jeans ripped apart. Fresh blood was cleaning the dirt away from her knees. Tears were filling her eyes and steadily got up on her legs, feeling all the round rocks under her bare feet. Her legs were hurting as her right cheeks got scratched all over. Her stomach was aching more and more and she was holding in the vomit that was fighting to come out. The taste in her mouth got worse. The darkness was rising, the clean and cold morning air was moving the top leaves. Her throat was burning and then, she could see the last round of trees in front of her. She hurried and close to her, she saw the last row of bushes standing out. She put her foot out on the cold sand. The waves beating the shore.

The cold blue sky above her was cleaning up. She was out. She kneeled down, embracing herself without controlling her unknown melancholy and let it come out. Spat the vomit taste out, some of it drained down her lip on the sweater.

Her washed out blond hair was blowing over her face. She crawled closer to the water and listened to the waves. The grief was coming back to her and she kept looking behind.

Took off her white shirt. The sweater. Her jeans which were so stretched out that they fell off, uncovering her legs. She took a smoke and held it in her dried left hand, between her slim fingers.

Looked down at her dirty bloody toes in the cold wet sand.

I have my feet cold since I can remember.

She was closer to entering the water, holding the broken cigarette but a repeated sound was becoming stronger and stronger. She could feel the cold water running over her ankles. The sky was turning grey. She fell on her knees and let the broken smoke out of her hand to be taken away by the waves.

Beep. Beep.

The sound was louder and wouldn't stop.

Beep. The sound…

She stayed still, facing the circular moving waves hitting her legs.

Beep. Beep. BEEP!

She was still fighting it. Her breath was uncontrollable. She could finally feel the real cold. The sound was so close to her that she could feel it behind her, hitting the back of her neck. Her chest felt like it was smashed to the ground, pressed hard against it. Her hands went numb and she would realize the numbness of her feet. Her hands touched the water. The taste was back on the top of her tongue. She was holding the necklace in her palm. The small round green stone was calming her.

Beep.

The sound almost woke her up completely.

The cold waves turned to dirt. She saw the long path behind the alley. The traffic light from the intersection was working again. Her blond hair felt, getting shorter. The dark curls covering her bloody checks. The light was yellow. It was green. It was red.

A heavy palm smashed over the neck hitting the right ear. 'Help! Somebody.'

Beep… Beep.

Second Part

20 Bucks and a Cigarette Pack

1

My numb half-opened eye was facing the reflection of a traffic light which somewhere before dawn stopped switching and remained yellow. Two papers of five bucks were taken away by the wind passing me. In my left dried hand, I had a broken cigarette from the last seven in the pack while my right was stuck under my body after trying to unzip my jeans. I remember coming out of the bowling alley when after a few minutes I was lying on the cold ground tasting the vomit inside my mouth.

He was a decent guy, my old man. He was tall and strong, with a charming look in his eyes. Father used to wear these shades of dark blue almost all the time. He would always nod and smile at the silly childish stories I came up with. Letting him know about my adventure times in the backyard garden. His cooking was awful, breaking the eggs for the 6 p.m. omelet in the cold oil from the pan and waiting for it to heat up. I was moving my plate around and looked at the leaking oil that was dripping into my floral plate.

'All the way down,' he said, laughing at me.

Father was quiet, cooking breakfast in the evening with no music on while I was sitting at the small round table playing with the fork and making odd sounds. At the end of the day, he was closing the curtains in my bedroom before going to sleep. It was the only bedroom from our apartment and he did not even once come and sleep next to me in my one-person bed (there was no room for another). He was sitting in his old sofa chair in silence all the night through, smelling funny. He would not take me with him on the long roads but sometimes, I would find myself next to my father. For hours, passing from one station to another. I was tall enough to see above the steering wheel, out the large front window. The two heavy parallel lines were sliding fast beneath the wheels of the moving train and I was trying to catch them with my eyes. The air inside the cabin was warm and sweat was falling off our armpits. I was going out and returning, moving in the shaking corridors when trying to hold my equilibrium on one foot. Dad was having a big smile on his face when I would return and start asking a lot of questions.

'What is that button do, Dad? Is your butt not hurting from sitting so long? Why does that lady have so much luggage, Dad? Can you turn the train around and go home with it? Why you always keep so many pills around? Can we take a seat from the train and put it in my bedroom?' I used to ask.

Father was laughing so hard at some of them. With tears in his eyes was patiently answering to each of them. His route was mostly the same, at least when he would take me, around the villages of the town. Father knew every broken or dried out or blooming tree on his way. Each field and what was growing on them, every passing station from the outside and guessing who was on duty in there. His favorite spot from all was this one path beneath some branches.

'Early in the morning Aaron, the sparkling sunlight is falling into the cabin in a million pieces through the leaves, son.'

It was warming you for two minutes until passing through the 'green' tunnel; as father called it. At the sound of the old and new branches hitting and sliding against the windows. The top ones, my dad told me, had these tiny pinkish flowers with very sensitive petals which on windy days were blown away and fell when passing. Some of them would be stuck on the large front window.

'You want me to slow down when passing, son?'

And he would, for me, so I could spin around on my toes like trying to catch the flying petals.

'Slowly now or you'll get dizzy.' Father was worrying too much sometimes. I knew I couldn't catch none, we were inside.

Arriving at a busier station, my father would have a cigarette with a red filter with the guy working that day. They were doing small talk about mostly their work and I was petting the dogs around the station.

'You're done soon?'

'Yeah, couple of minutes and I'm out.'

'We had a delay in the morning. There was an accident and the cops closed the road. There where cars stuck on the lines,' he said between smokes.

'Yes, we know. It didn't affect this part too much but on the west side there were a lot of complaints.'

The end of the conversation will be about something even more insignificant.

'Will warm up next week again.'

'Oh yeah?' Father threw away the cigarette. 'Aaron, we gotta go. Come, boy.'

The day will come to an end and we would return. Father will turn into the smelly vegetable in the chair until sunrise.

The evening was close, I remember; father was making extra hours for Christmas presents; buying me the new bicycle model. The one each child from the neighborhood wanted. We did not have space nor the money for a big, beautiful Christmas tree, but we would together catch up some old lights next to the curtains and put the paper decorations (that Aaron made in school each year) on the window and kitchen chairs. The days back then seemed deserted and longer without Father by my side. There were days in a week passing and not seeing him. Our apartment looked bigger but quiet. The weather outside began being more unfriendly for some, but not for me. I remember looking out the rainy window waiting for him to get home. Sometimes he would come earlier, sometimes he wouldn't. From time to time, singing the alphabet song I knew wouldn't bother him at all. It was a peaceful place when he would rush right inside in his dark soaked uniform from the rain. The floor was making a song of my every step when wandering around the living room with a bunch of clothes on; Aaron was opening every drawer, shaking the yellow containers with his father's name tag on it and put them back. His tiny pants were tighter up with one of the shoelaces of his father's shoe so it wouldn't feel down while running on the narrow corridor with the doors opened between; his numb arms stretched out. The wooden floor was beaten with the jumping steps and the murmuring sounds of Aaron copying a helicopter.

He was trying to walk forward to the kitchen in the bigger-sized shoes, dragging them after him and lifting the edges of the coat so he won't step on it. In the opened space living room, Aaron's father caught up three of his plane models which looked like always moving. One of the models had the white lateral lines of the wings uniformly covered in a light blue color; with one pen Aaron found in the station lobby while waiting for his father. Outside the window, the stormy wind stopped and peacefully the snowflakes were falling down soon after. Aaron would stay for hours looking out at how gently the layers of snow grew bigger. Drinking water from the dirty coffee smelling mug. Often falling asleep and getting carried into bed at his father's return. Aaron stayed next to him during the entire night. Getting scared at his dad's snoring which sounded like choking him.

In the beginning, Aaron was looking through the cracked door then ending at the left side of his brown leather imitation sofa, which they both found one day in the corner of a supermarket and brought it back with them. Aaron walked slowly on his toes closing his eyes at the loud, as he was hearing it at that moment, floor. Wearing his aviator pajamas. The smoke from the room was hurting his eyes, making him forcefully shut his tiny green eyes and then wait for a while until he won't see blurry anymore. His father numbly holding a cigarette which seemed that smoked by itself, with the ash holding on together. The ashtray was full, putting out one cigarette on top of another, one filter by another. Around the mess, the smoke was rising to the ceiling covering it with a light grey mist. His father looked, in the poor light from the corner lamp with the shadow covering half his face, like he aged within one whole week. Aaron kneeled down and before realizing he was sleeping with his head on the sofa arm.

Aaron opened his eyes on a school day. The holidays were over. His father for as long as he could remember was never in his room. This time he was looking over him from the edge of the bed.

'Go pack boy,' Father said barely moving his lips.

The young boy got dressed and ready for school. Aaron stayed in front of his father who got back on his sofa. Whose saliva was leaking down his chest at his lost look. The empty shaking bottles from the top of the refrigerator were in rhythm with the ticking clock. Aaron did not move nor make a sound in front of him. He was controlling his breathing.

Father?

Aaron was holding with both hands the tiny school bag with books heavier than him. A smell hit Aaron, another then the usual funny one from the opened bottles. In the kitchen sink, he went to look covering his nose with the school uniform sleeve. It was a heavy piece of meat drowned in its own blood and cold water, from the melted ice cubes. It was blocking the drain and the smell of rotten meat scared Aaron.

The front door cracked open letting the cold inside. Several heavy steps echoed the living room. Then the boots stooped. Aaron let go of the school backpack and ran screaming into Mr. Jackson's arms.

'Grandpa,' Aaron giggled.

The snow from the top of his shoes was melting. Mr. Jackson took Aaron in his arms lifting him so he could touch the ceiling.

'Did you pack, boy?'

Aaron nodded pointing at his school bag.

'No, but clothes boy. Did you pack those?' Mr. Jackson said with the hesitation of looking towards the sofa.

Aaron did not.

'Want me to help you?' he smiled showing all his teeth.

'Yes,' Aaron continued to giggle and put his tiny arms around Mr. Jackson's covered neck.

Holding his grandfather's hand by two fingers, they both went into Aaron's room to pack. Mr. Jackson avoiding to look at his son from the sofa with the corner of his eye gently followed the boy in front of him.

'Where we going?' Aaron wondered.

'You will stay at my place for a while. You boy will love it. Just yesterday the children from the village put all this snow together to make a…'

'Father? We pack his clothes too?' the child said while pushing his shirts in a bag.

Mr. Jackson took a deep breath and kneeled.

'Your father needs to be alone now.'

'But why? Why can't he be alone with us?'

'Look,' Mr. Jackson put his hand on Aaron's shoulder. 'He has to be alone. And he will have to return to work at some point.'

The smell of the rotten meat passed the smoke smelling living room until the boy's bedroom.

'Why can't he work from where you live, Grandpa?' Aaron's eyes begin shining.

‘Shhh,’ Mr. Jackson said with a heavy breath. ‘We can’t talk about it now. Your, your father needs to get fine and we will help.’

‘Father’s sick?’

‘A little bit. But it’s not how you would think. Listen, boy. He’s going on vacation and he’ll get better.’

‘He’s going? Where is Father going, Grandpa? I wanna go too. I wanna go with him!’

‘Our vacation starts now boy. He’ll come after, all right?’

Aaron nodded and finished packing. He dropped in the shoelaces he used as a belt when left alone.

Mr. Jackson covered his nose when passing through the living room with quick steps, pushing the kid in front of him.

Aaron stopped near his father to look at him.

‘See ya, Dad. We’re going on a vacation.’ He lost his smile soon at the reaction of his father not moving at all. He did move his eyeballs away from Aaron’s look. ‘We wait for you Dad, okay?’ Aaron was caressing his father’s arm.

‘Dad?’ Tears were running down his pink cheeks.

Mr. Jackson grabbed the boy and turn him around. With a judgmental face, he looked at his son and pushed Aaron in front of him to the front door.

‘Dad?’ Aaron screamed. He was nervous and wanted to run back when Mr. Jackson took him in his arms.

‘We have to leave now,’ Mr. Jackson seriously said.

It was work and nothing else left for him, but me. His uniform messy and sweaty each time he would return and while forcing himself into taking a shower, he was always starting the washing machine first. My olive-green aviator pajamas, that stopped being soft after too many washes were spinning around among his dark blue pants. I remember that last scream, the way Mr. Jackson's heavy arms lifted me up, away from the sight of my own father.

The floor behind them was covered by the watery footsteps from Mr. Jackson's boots. Aaron looked back at his father, seeing him decomposing in the rotten meat smell.

Aaron's quick and silent steps were holding up to Mr. Jacksons in the cold weather. They both walked holding hands without any words. His neck was covered around by a dark blue scarf with bigger white and then few red stripes. The few tears that escaped were turning cold because of the violent wind that was blowing from ahead. The kid's shoulders were so down that the backpack from his back wouldn't stay on. It fell on his arms, he continued to walk and Mr. Jackson took it off and carried it in his right hand. Arrived at the bus station Aaron's cheeks and nose turned red. He looked down at his moving feet that could not stay still and were playing in the snow. Aaron was holding back his tears by biting his tongue until this warm salty taste filled his mouth. The world around him was peaceful. He was lost in his thoughts.

'Ya hnho h'a sthroh.' Aaron heard the words like out of a bag. His head did not raise but he felt the squeeze of his hand. It was Mr. Jackson trying to comfort him.

'You're not a kid anymore, boy,' Mr. Jackson said looking upon Aaron.

2

The first skin layer of the left cheek and from the top of the nose was stuck to the ground. The upper lip was smashed and my slightly turned head was lying in a light combination of vomit and blood. The smell of it surrounding me. I am glad I didn't bite my tongue off.

Our farm was small. Nothing seemed to ever grow around. But green fields as far as one could see. There was a line of not so tall and skinny trees on one side of the wooden cabin. Mr. Jackson used to walk along them as often as he could. Back and front. When I first arrived, after the long road we had, the place looked like in a rush cleaning. Windows with soapy marks left on them where, because of my tiny height, I was only seeing a blurry shadow of myself. Dust behind the plates, unfolded blankets and bags with useless stuff in one corner of the room. We would share one bed for the first year. Mr. Jackson rolling and putting a blanket between the space of the bed and wall so I wouldn't feel the cold so badly. The smell of food was always filling the cabin. Under the table, in the middle of the room, were two close to each other used carpets where I was playing in the wintertime with the corn. Building forts as high as I could, sometimes if not busy with the fire, Mr.

Jackson would hold them for me and I would put more on the top. At the same table on my green repainted chair, which grandfather let me paint, I was eating a cup with hot milk and soak bread in the morning; then Mr. Jackson would look upon me when going to the village school. I would meet with Mathew and race until the gates of the school. Mr. Jackson had a heavy chair in one corner with a homemade pillow on it where he would occasionally fall asleep. When returning from school in the afternoon, the middle table was covered in flour and I was sweeping the carpet under it to help out. We would mostly eat cabbage soup and pasta with potatoes or pasta with warm milk over it. On Sunday we would have some piece of baked cake with poppy seeds and honey which would be enough through the week.

The following spring, after all the snow has melted, I woke up early one day and got dressed for playing outside. Having a pair of plastic glasses running down my nose, I keep pushing them up with the back of my hand so it would stop sliding. I was carefully pushing aside the dried tree branches with small black round circles at the end of them. Looking through them glasses, the close mist dancing at the bottom of the tree roots turned purple, turned blue, turned cold. I straightened up my curved back and almost choked on the deep cold breath I rushed to take. My tiny muddy finger was glued to the middle of the glasses. Still holding the pair up my red nose. The white ball on the distant sky, that I couldn't look at for too long before my eyes would be filled with tears at the corners, was like running on my right side with me. The cracks of dried uncovered branches from the ground were smashed under my heavy rubber boots. My arm stretched out ahead of me so that I could wipe down with my sleeve the spider webs that keep sticking onto my warmed-up face. I couldn't see my breath while running but only after stopping. It was a warm air coming fast out of my mouth. My eyeballs spinning like crazy around, to my left and right, rising to the top of the trees and far to the steady warm clouds. I walked under a fallen thick branch avoiding the bushes which were full of thorns and got out from the small forest near the path. From where I was standing, I could see Mr. Jackson. He had his head covered and got a pair of gloves which were cut at the fingers. Boots until the knee covering his muddy pants and a yellow and brown striped sweater. Hands hanging near the body with the sleeves falling down. One leg lifted and staring to a cut root tree which was spited over by the red dripping blood.

My shadow on the opened field was twice as long as I actually was at the time. I walked looking down at my funny moving body, barely scratched palm but holding and raising my green cotton pants for Mr. Jackson to see from far away.

'What you did there, boy?'

I was all the way until down there a courageous boy who was more fascinated by his own shadow and didn't even realized the cuts on his knee and palms. But hearing Mr. Jackson's voice my eyes turned watery and my dusty chin shook.

'Now, now. Come here. Let's take a closer look at it,' his eyes were smiling at me.

My left leg was covered with salty blood running down. Olive green and dark purple bruises showing up already. He stepped aside from the rabbit which was dangling over, caught by one foot and let the animal dry out of blood.

Mr. Jackson went and come back holding a young tree trunk. His hands had mud on them and he smiling, told me to go help him. This made me forget about my bleeding knee. He digs a tiny round hole in the middle of his favorite path and we rushed back there. I was walking near his side still holding up my pants over the bruises. He put the root in the hole and told me to hold it with both hands. I let go and my boot got covered by the falling pants. He kneeled down and with his bare hands pushed the fresh smelly earth back uniformly, covering the root.

'Don't have to hold it anymore.' He smiled touching the ground, keeping his palm against it for a while. Mr. Jackson stood. 'It will grow old with me if God intends.'

* *

Years passed since my grandfather showed up at the front door of our apartment and I could still sometimes if concentrating hard enough feel the smell of rotten meat in my nose and taste it in my mouth. *You're not a kid anymore.* The words of Mr. Jackson were echoing in my dreams and sometimes early in the mornings.

'It ain't always like this,' Mr. Jackson said from his chair while chewing on a piece of bread crust. 'Before ya was born, me and your grandmother were all day long, since the sunrise till darkness on those fields, boy. Sweating down our foreheads in the strong sun with only a cap covering our heads. You know, your grandmother knew how to cook. Better than me even. Oh my, and what kind of cooking. In the afternoon when the sun was the strongest, we put a blanket on the path right there,' he pointed to the trees out the window. 'And she would make a hell of a lunch. She put down some homemade fresh bread with goat cheese and sweet tomatoes. You should have tasted her pumpkin pie boy. If I close my eyes, I could still taste a piece of its flavor.' Mr. Jackson started to laugh with shiny eyes. 'Damn pies she used to make.'

He was falling asleep in his chair while still talking, then confusedly wake up and continue.

'On Sunday mornings if you would walk for 20 minutes right there, around the corner, we were a hand of man selling what growing to the passing cars and exchanging with one another. The old man Travis from across the road came one morning with a bunch of strawberries to give. He gave me some for a bag of dried sunflower seeds. In cold nights to eat those with salt and some olive oil mixed in a pan was more than what you needed.' He paused and broke the bread in smaller pieces. 'I ran back here to show your grandmother. She mixed them and put those in pancakes after coming from church. I myself was never too religious. And she did not ask for going with her besides Christmas Eve and Easter. She liked the idea of being together on those nights in front of an altar. Was never able to understand why, but I loved how her face lit up when I was by her side.'

'In a world where religion is taboo, we have to understand that heaven is the purgatory we created,' Aaron said.

'Ya right boy,' Mr. Jackson said before falling asleep. The slice of bread fell out his hand, Aaron took it and put it on the table.

Aaron spent the rest of the night on the top of his bed looking at Mr. Jackson. His breath was getting heavier, his hands were going numb, his stomach was itchy, and he felt something staying in his neck. Longer he was watching the old man, the worse his state got. The image of the peaceful but tired man asleep brought him back in his old apartment. Right before leaving for a vacation.

Father. Aaron got up and got closer to Mr. Jackson. Kneeled in front of him in silence. The time passed. Mr. Jackson started to snore and Aaron was wearing a red sweater when he decided to say goodbye. He went to touch his hand but didn't dare. Not if it could be a possibility of waking him up. Instead, he kept his hand above the old man's, at a close distance for a while. He then turned around and begin putting clothes in one of his backpacks. Mr. Jackson was following him from his chair. Making sure he's not seen by Aaron. He opened the backpack and just by grabbing some clothes he threw them inside. He was looking to leave a note on the table but changed his mind. He put Mr. Jackson's big sweater from the bed. Took the backpack and the green sneakers in his hands and went to the door. A quick look behind at Mr. Jackson in his chair. (Thinking that he doesn't know that his boy is leaving). *I'm sorry but I gotta go now. Thank you.* Aaron slowly opened the door with unsteady hands because of the click of the door. Touching the lucky coin Mr. Jackson gave him as a child. The one that will give him strength. Got outside and easily in the beginning went towards the path where he stopped to put his sneakers on. He did flip the coin in the air, catching it, then put it in his back pocket. The smell of the trees hit him and while tying the shoelaces he put his hand on the dried ground and felt how he's getting nervous again. Aaron wanted to look back at the cabin but did not dare. He got up. The sun was not far from rising. The sky was steady. The path he stood on was longer in front of him than it ever was. It was quiet. He breathed on his mouth. Holding his chest. Curling his toes. The pain got stronger along with his desire of getting away. Everything has an ending. He holds his breath and then starts running as fast as he could straight up the path. Two drops were racing down his cheeks while running and then a smile was covering his face. His mouth corners arched and curved from one ear to another. The faster he ran, the more relief he felt.

'Ohuuw, aah.'

Aaron got on the road and ran in the middle of it until he couldn't feel his legs anymore, his chest was hurting just like something was pressing it, his burning sweat was falling and then he ran faster. Laughing his heart out and shouting with his hands above his head at the following noise of the backpack hitting against his rushed back. He was getting away. He was leaving.

Mr. Jackson got up from his chair after Aaron left. 'I saw you boy.' He went and took the boy's blanket and covered himself, put it on his shoulders and held it with one hand as close to his face as to feel his scent. 'Saw you becoming him over the years.' He waited a while and then opened the cabin's door. He stayed even there under the verge of the door. Laughing when hearing joy screaming coming from far away. He was laughing with Aaron. His shaking body waited for the sun rising up above the tall trees from the path. Mr. Jackson closed his eyes and breathed in the clean and chill air. The smile was not missing from his face. He tasted his tears while the sunlight was brightening his old pale face.

'Good luck boy.'

Aaron was keeping his path on the road. Within a couple of hours, he found himself out. He left the countryside behind and walked forward.

3

There were a couple of deposit storages behind the bowling alley with a large unlit and humid path between. The strong white headlights from a parked car were blinding me, I remember, when the door slammed by my back and I tried taking a smoke out of the packet. I could hear the loud cars passing by; not stopping at the traffic light. My stomach was always almost empty by the time I start pouring beer, at first, in it. The large street still awake. At the intersection, the colors were changing. Now red, now yellow, now green. My right hand stuck under my body has gone numb. The surface of my vomit close to my face got as dry as my cracked lips and my half-opened eye was beaten by the changing reflected colors.

He was not rushing anymore but his heartbeats were still racing. He saw no one since he left but passing trucks coming from ahead. Aaron turned his head at the speeding sound. Hoop up his backpack on his shoulder and straighten up his hand. He put the weight in both his feet and waited with the smoke in the corner of his mouth.

'Where to?' a voice said from the slowing car which stopped before him.

'Away.'

‘Away is where I’m going. Need a ride?’

Aaron jumped, opening the red door of the car and let his backpack on the back seat. Closing the door, he looked back at the long fields he left behind.

‘Noah.’ A man close to his age was loudly chewing on a piece of melon taste gum.

‘Aaron.’

‘How long were you walking for?’

‘Not long, been running a big part of it,’ Aaron said while strangling his soaked armpits.

‘Troubles at home?’

Aaron stared at him for a moment.

‘I remember when I ran away for four days just after we all run out of money and went back like nothing ever happened. Our parents were so worried they didn’t do much about it. Hell with it, for one chick, her folks seemed to be more disappointed for her going back. It’s just, you know, you don’t see many people walking near the road at this time in the morning.’

‘No problems,’ Aaron hesitated. ‘Guess the old man is too tired to pick up a fight.’

‘Then you’re lucky. Mine, pfft, always trying to introduce me to some sort of, I don’t even know man,’ Noah laughed. ‘Some partners of his and when I finally accepted, he yelled at me in front of others because my shirt was not tucked in my goddamn pants. Can you believe it? One of the corners was hanging out after I took a piss and he lost it big time.’ Noah stopped and turned to Aaron, waiting for a smile. ‘Well, all good now, I caught him fingering one of the old redheads from his office. No need to work no more, let me tell you that,’ he proudly said it.

Aaron's foot repeatedly got hit by a rolling empty can.

'So what's your old man doing then?'

'I live with his father,' Aaron said under his breath.

'Hmmm, never met mine. They died while Camelia was pregnant with my bigger sister.'

'I never knew my mother.'

'You grew up with your grandfather then?'

'He took me away a long time ago,' Aaron said while stepping on the empty can so it would stop rolling.

'Took you away?' Noah's voice got higher.

'Long time ago. Yes.' Aaron looked over at Noah who was staring ahead. It was a conversation long waited for him, beside Mr. Jackson. 'I did leave with my father but, you see, I never knew why he used to smell so bad and I never asked him or myself.'

The silence grew in the car as did Noah's enthusiasm for hearing more of the story, and he turned off the radio so he could listen to Aaron.

'It was just him. What made him my father? His strong smell. That's how I knew he was near me. Even when he thought I was asleep. It was awful.' Aaron laughed. 'I used to hug him even tighter, you know.'

For some reason, Aaron felt freedom. Talking about his old man freely without worrying about Mr. Jackson.

'That's why you live with your grandfather? Because your father liked drinking too much?' Noah asked.

'He didn't like it,' Aaron defended him. 'My father was sick. Alcohol was his salvation and he was nothing but kind to me. He couldn't take the depression anymore.'

'I'm sorry man. Didn't meant to upset you or anything. I think that you know, those kind of people are selfish, just as my own man. Don't care about what happens around. They just see the bottle in front of them or a new pair of legs and that's the most important thing.'

Aaron moved uncomfortably in his chair.

'I guess so.' His look got lost on the white lines he was running near the road not long ago.

'All I'm saying is they have no worry in this big goddamn world.' His chewing got louder and his constant eyebrows raising after each sentence played awfully in Aaron's left sight.

'Can you stop the car?'

'Oh, come on, man. You brought it up, haven't you?'

'Nothing like that, I think I got far enough, thank you.'

'My father was the same,' Noah said while taking his foot off the accelerator. 'He never did anything for me. Missed everything around him. When I graduated, he asked me how old I was, he had no clue about anything, ever. Yelling out his own frustration was the best thing he knew how to do.'

'My old man was not like that.'

'But he did give up on you, right?'

'He did what he thought was right at that time.'

The car stopped and Noah turned the radio on from which a low static sound was coming in.

'Well. have a nice one,' he said, bending closer to Aaron.

'He wasn't selfish. He was sick and he called to come after me. He knew I'll be in good hands,' Aaron stayed in his seat to explain, then politely closed the door after taking his backpack from the back seat. Aaron wanted for some reason to slam it as hard as he could and wished that he had never started that conversation.

Aaron was thinking of going back. Maybe all this was a mistake. *I'll be back soon.*

He did not get too far from where he was. He kept his path on the road after the red car was getting smaller and smaller in front of his eyes and did not take another ride. He'll arrive close to the evening next to a lighthouse.

He got away from the road when he heard in the distance the sound of waves hitting the shore. The powerful orange sky from that morning disappeared long ago, once with the deserted fields. He walked against the wind with his backpack in his arm. His pale skin looked whiter in the blue skylight. The small trees around there were skinnier than him and he was holding the edge of the red sweater in his long fingers, dragging its sleeves on the sand.

In front of Aaron was an old man smoking outside with a hat covering his ears and the back of his thick neck. His black pants were folded up over his ankles and he was moving his toes up and down in the cold, wet sand. The old man was moving slowly ahead with his feet in the water, then he stopped and waited for the calm waves to come. He was scratching his forehead with his darkened uncut fish smelling nails and looked far in the distance before seeing Aaron who was looking at him.

On the sand were a pile of branches and what seems like dried thorn-surrounded bushes put together over one another. Aaron walked closer to them. The old man jumped when seeing him. He was looking amazed at him while his soaked feet were covered by the circling waves.

The old man's eyes got bigger and a smile rounded in the corner of his mouth.

'Well, good evening young fella.' The old man was almost running toward Aaron, looking down trying to clean the sticky sand off his feet. 'I don't see many people around here.' His hand was wide open to shake him. 'It's usually me and my loud thoughts and to be honest, almost can't stand each other no more,' he said.

Aaron's muscles relaxed at the old man's welcoming.

'I saw the lighthouse when I walked through the path and though it might be something around here.'

'It is always an old man waiting for some company here.' The old man searched his pockets for his smoke pack and held it to Aaron. 'Take one.'

'Oh thank you but I have my own.' Aaron did not have the time to finish talking before the old man took out his matches also.

'Hmmm, thank you.'

The old man put his hands together so that Aaron could light up his smoke.

'I'm sorry. It's been 17 days since I last talked to someone,' he said while stepping back and lighting up a cigarette for himself.

'I needed a break from the road.'

'Long one?'

'Pretty much. At least it feels like.'

'Vacation, young man?'

Aaron took a deep breath and looked far at the horizon.

'Aye. The waves are quiet today. Last Tuesday, young man, there was a strong storm. I had to take all those broken branches and put them in that pile over there.' He pointed at the pile Aaron passed by.

He remembered that day. He was walking back to the farm between the tall trees when the heavy drops of rain got to him. He arrived soaked in front of the cabin but not went inside. He first undressed and squeezed his clothes and put them on the edge of the wooden balcony. He turned and looked away to the far trees which got a slight white color on their top branches because of the mist. In front of him, the rain was falling strongly down like a moving curtain, hitting the mud that formed on the bottom of the stairs.

Aaron was following the back of the brown sweater the old man was wearing.

The huge image of a pelican glued to a plastic frame over the table, stuck to the wall, caught his eyes. It was hanging on one side by a nail, ready to fall any moment. The lifted covers of dozens of books under the window were raised upon from the bend pages. It was later when he saw the books actually staying on top of puzzle boxes. Between the glasses, he spotted something unusual. It was a small statue of Madonna in a white dress. He could tell it was an old one because of the fallen pieces from its face and arms.

He sat on the cold wooden chair at the table. The old man was bringing the glasses in his shaking hands, making them hit each other constantly. In his round grey hall, the clicking was echoing up the stairs and back.

'There ya go, young man. Just as old as I am.' The old man smiled with his eyes. 'It's been a while since someone stayed in that chair ya know.' He lowered his look, sighed and dragged a chair next to Aaron. As close as he could taste his breath.

'Thank you.' Aaron took the glass and smelled it while the old man swallowed the whole thing. He took the bottle and filled it up again.

'So tell me. Why is a young man like you wandering alone in these parts?'

Aaron put the glass down on the edge of the table still holding it and look up at the old man who put his hat lower on his forehead.

'I, I was.' Aaron was asking that himself since he left.

The old man seemed like waiting to stop laughing so he could talk.

'Aye. When I was your age, my dear boy, I had not a clue about where or what I was doing neither. Don't worry, you will know when you find it.'

'I had no good reason to leave. It just felt right.'

'Aha, aha.' The old man nodded approving. 'Getting away for a while you say?'

'Yes. Going away.'

'Well, I'm glad you did.' The old man dragged the bottle closer so he could fill up Aarons glass which he did not finish drinking yet. 'I get pretty lonely around these parts. An old man like me needs company to talk with.'

'I was talking with Mr. Jackson quite a bit. He would not stop talking if you ask me.' They both start laughing. 'Mr. Jackson is my grandfather.'

'You do? You do talk to him?' he asked, surprised. 'Aye, my son nor nephew won't come by. They say they're way too busy to come and see an old man like myself.' He drank up and looked at the empty glass.

'I could never talk about my mother with my father and yet never talked about my father with Mr. Jackson.'

‘Aye, looks like none of us were able to talk then.’

They both stayed with their looks fixed on the glasses for a while.

‘I say let’s drink to that.’ The old man’s eyes were bigger and shinier than before. His gaze was warm when leaning back on his chair with the raised glass. ‘We as individuals need companionship or we lose it. Look at me boy.’ His voice got heavier. ‘I’m 62 years old and all day long I’m waiting for my son to return my calls. The days are quiet but the nights, pfft, they are the worst. As you get older young man you can’t sleep no more. Can’t rest. Even when my son calls back, he is always in a rush to hang up.’

They both finished their glasses and in no time, the old man filled them up again.

Outside, the weather got cold and the night arrived. Inside the rounded kitchen, the bottle got lighter with every poured glass. The cold was not a problem behind the closed door for them. The sound of the dragging glasses over the wooden table was partially covering the sound of the waves hitting the shore.

‘I remember her just from the photos. Father never talked about her with me or anyone else. I saw she had dark hair and green eyes. I couldn’t get why father used to look at me with sad eyes when he thought I am not looking. Until I saw that. It was this photograph I found at Mr. Jackson a few years ago with her and my father at a Christmas party. She was wearing a black dress, holding a pair of heels in her hand and had blond short hair back then. She still looked healthy back there. Her lips were turning black from too much red wine and my father holding her tight. On her dress was resting an old golden necklace with a small green stone in the middle. I don't remember from where she had it but she was always wearing it,' Aaron said while the old man fixed his hat over his ears, dragging it down with two thick fingers.

'Maybe it was to be that way. After I lost my Mary, my son left me two years after. Just after he turned 18. He used to call at the beginning before he got too busy for me.'

'I will go back. I just felt like going away for a while. Get out of the farm.'

'I'm sure he understands, young man. I did. I still would and do. But listen to me, boy. Listen carefully. Don't wait too much until you go back,' the old man said having a slight regret in his voice. 'We all grow up and want to leave. Some of us forget from where we left and that is the end of it.'

'We always return from where we left,' Aaron continued.

'And I'm sure you will young man.' He stood up to empty the ashtray. 'Let me ask you something. Did you leave to go see your father?'

Aaron straightened up in his warmed-up chair. It was obvious he was not waiting for that question.

'I thought about it for a long time over the years but,' he heavily swallowed.

'So you're already not returning. See what I'm talking about?'

'The only time Mr. Jackson talked with me about him was when he told me he has moved away. I was not that young to not understand that they took him away. Maybe put him in a clinic to get some help or something. Never actually asked more about it.'

'You're a good man. I can tell. Don't ever hesitate to ask. You never know how the ending will be after all. You never know.'

'The most painful ending is that which we don't see,' Aaron said.

'That is true, young man,' the old man giggled softly, already red in his cheeks from the alcohol. 'Here, let me fill that up for you.'

It was half-past two in the morning but none of them knew the time. They drank the whole bottle and smoked a full pack of smokes until they had time to realize it. The night was quiet and the water calm. The room ceiling was covered in a slight mist of Lucky Strike smokes before the old man got up to go open the window. The cold air coming inside woke them both.

Aaron realized the time that had passed and got up to leave.

'Oh but it's no problem. I enjoy talking to you, young man. I have another bottle in the back that I didn't open yet. You're more than welcome to stay. Here, sit down.' The old man pushed Aaron's shoulder to sit him back in his chair. He then went looking in the back, hitting slightly with his almost dried shock that he put over his wet feet the lined boxes from the back. He stopped at the sound of one clink. Pushed his palm against the carton box and took out the bottle of gin. The old man came back with another bottle as he said. One could tell it was sitting there for a while because of the dust that was covering it.

'Let me ask you. I told you about the nephew I have. You know, he owns this bowling thing down in the town. Well, more like near, the edge of the town but he told me he had to stay late one night last week because… I don't remember what happened.'

Aaron lit up a smoke while the old man was trying to pour another glass for each of them. Some which spilled on the table and was running down the floor.

'What I'm trying to say is, that if you are looking for a place to make some easy money, I can always give him a call in the morning and ask for you.' The old man dragged his foot to wipe the gin from the floor.

Aaron's eyes brightened up when hearing the old man and not just because of the warm liquor running through his veins. It would be his first job besides taking care of the farm and would be more than perfect to return with some money back to Mr. Jackson. The excuse Aaron was looking for, he had found it.

'I know between what time to call him in the morning so that he would answer.' The old man saw Aaron's face brighten up and promised that he would talk with his nephew the first thing in the morning but not before they would drink another one.

The first thing in the morning the old man called his nephew, the one he was complaining about that he is all the time too busy to visit, as he promised Aaron the night before. Talked to him for about 12 minutes, more than they usually do and got Aaron the job.

He put over his brown sweater a leather vest he once found on the edge of the road and went on his small round chair from outside and waited for Aaron to wake up so he could give him the good news. The sky was blooming in its orange clouds from above the water once again.

Aaron woke up in the steady chair at the smell of fish oil dripping off one plate in the kitchen sink, after two more hours while the old man was making no noise outside. The grey hall was different in the sunlight. The walls were, in fact, beige and not white as he had thought. He got up with a headache but the objects from around the kitchen were not moving anymore. Rinsed the glass from the table and let the cold water run. Outside the lighthouse, Aaron saw the old man with his hat over his eyes smoking a cigarette.

'How you feeling boy?' the old man asked without turning his head. He had heard his steps from inside.

Aaron wanted to laugh but pressed his forehead against the cold glass instead. 'Long night.'

'Come, sit. Want me to bring another glass of gin?' the old man said joking around.

'Oh no. All good.'

'You still have to learn young man. Wanna know my secret? Can't be hungover if you're drunk,' the old man said pulling up his hat and give a funny look to Aaron.

Aaron remained silent and continued to drink his water.

'Talked to my nephew. You have it if you want.'

After the sky lost its orange color the old man called back so Aaron could talk with Vrye, but not before the two smoked cigarettes.

Aaron left on the same path as he came. This time waving back to the smiling old man who was waving holding his hat in his hand. His left white hair around his ears beat slowly by the kind wind.

Not far from the bowling alley, Aaron will find a cheap apartment to rent.

4

The top branches of the trees were moving but the wind didn't seem unfriendly. From above, my fainted body in the middle of the path had my legs forming this curvy "P". Not so far is a running out light bulb hung with uncovered wires. Making my skin look sickening. With that amount of alcohol in your body, it was just about time until one will start throwing it out again. The door, without hearing it, was getting opened and closed by the leaving people. Longer into the night, quieter it becomes. My left hand holding the broken cigarette starts bleeding between the cracks.

He easily found the bowling alley and went inside to talk with Vrye, the old man's nephew, but he was not at the place; called that morning and said he had something to take care of. An employee from behind the counter with the hair always running in his eyes was waiting for Aaron to show up and told him that Vrye will meet him at a bar not far from there. Told him how to find the place and Aaron was on his way.

The bar was a small place with usually the same people going in and out at the same hours. Calling each other names and gathered closely around the counter. Few of them resting in front of shiny screens from the machines with a glass in their left hand, pushing harder and harder on the buttons.

He went and sat at a round cheap plastic table covered with dragged rag marks and cigarette burns. He was the one sitting there in a while, he thought. The waitress wondering came over, followed by the turned heads from the counter. Brought him a glass and turned her back to him. Aaron was waiting for Vrye to show up and slid in his chair to the left so that he could see in the mirror whoever was entering the place.

Vrye was not much older than Aaron. Few years between the two. Later when he walked in the bar the switching neon lighting from above the bar and gambling machines were reflected in his shiny shoes. He was wearing black cotton pants with a way too big belt which was distinguished in the strong light. A purple shirt with its sleeves rolled up below his elbows and a silver watch constantly playing on his wrist while walking. His big brown eyes flickering under his bushy eyebrows and with a glint he caught Aaron's look in the mirror.

Suddenly, Aaron recognized the smell. His father used to smell like so all the time. Aaron dragged his glass closer to him just under his chin, enough for him to have his nose above the smell. Without the intention of drinking it but sniff it for as long as he could. It would be the only way he found in years of being closer to him again. The green moving light was falling on the transparent glass, unwilling all the fingerprints left on it and dirty lip stains. Aaron was gently moving his thumbs up and down that glass. Not taking his eyes off the waving liquor.

The music from inside the bar was fading apart in Aaron's ears by every minute until it was quiet at last. The lights were having no more color in his eyes. Around the glass, only shadow.

'You must be Aaron?' a close voice beside him confidently asked.

'Ah, yes. Yes, I am,' he replied.

The smell was like printed in his mind at that time. Aaron could taste it.

'Wednesdays are the worst in that place, I'm telling you. All those old folks competing every week over, to be honest, I don't even know,' Vrye said while moving the seat closer to Aaron. 'What you having over there?' He bent over the table to look into Aaron's glass. 'I see. I'll have the same then.' He waved his fingers into the air to catch the waitress attention and asked for a glass of absinthe. 'So then, I've heard you did nothing but farming before?'

'I was helping around yes.'

'Why leave then? Your old folks making you go crazy?'

'No. It was nothing,' Aaron did not have the time to finish because he was interrupted by Vrye.

'Take it as a joke. I used to help around also with a lot of things, you know.'

Aaron was nodding from time to time to the dark-haired man in front of him who was louder than all those at the bar together. Never resting his left arm and gesticulating a lot with strong movements of his fingers. Stretching his leg under the table then drag it back. Vrye had a way of touching his cheekbones with the top of his index finger when drinking. Playing with the smooth napkin under his glass when swallowing. Aaron learned to pay attention to

Vrye and sniff his memories at the same time by waving his chin above the glass.

Minutes passed and Aaron had time to study every inch of the liquor, could close his eyes and see it but the smell seemed to disappear. Aaron nervously took it and swallowed it all at once. Tears were leaking from the corner of his eyes while the burn in his throat calmed down; it was like kissing his father on the cheek again. Hugging him tighter while choking on the smell.

The long night trying his best to pay attention to Vrye passed and he was now heading to his first apartment where Vrye offered to show him the way. The business he had to take care of earlier that day; when Vrye first moved out there, he found himself an apartment in the same building he was bringing Aaron.

The place was not far from the bar which would be in Aaron's way to the bowling alley and the building. He was trying not to swallow too often so that the taste in his mouth will last longer. It was a straight road they both walked in silence for most of it, Vrye smoking his Phil Morris cigarette, and took a right turn at the end.

He pointed towards the building with the fingers he was holding the smoke. The building was an old warehouse. With one floor above, hot roof in the summer but cold walls in winter, a heavy green door with the painting peeled and deserted tall windows. From outside, it was only from one window that some light has shown any movement. And it seemed to be from the switching channels of a television closely placed near the corner of the room. First thing in the morning Vrye was to introduce him to an old friend of his;

the one owning the building. He threw away the cigarette butt and opened the iron door for Aaron.

He was still dizzy from the drink he hurried to swallow earlier. He walked closer to the hot walls of the narrow hall holding and checking the key he had between two fingers. Aaron stopped suddenly in front of the door and straightened his back as if preparing himself. Turning the silver key in the lock, he rolled back the whole tape from his mind until the point where he was now at the place. Looked back to salute Vrye and stepped inside. The sliding door closed gently behind him. The apartment was not brightened up. Through the tall windows, the streetlights brightened up the white and black small tiles, some of them cracked and some missing, being piled up in the bathtub. Window glass so dirty that the light would come in grey. He found the switching button close to the steel door. He then saw a brown sofa near a pillar. Aaron first threw the used sofa in one corner. The floor was still, not making a sound at his heavy clumsy steps and Aaron remembered sitting in the corner on his obliquely placed sofa, putting imaginary items all over the empty room. Over time it was true, he brought more stuff in his place, empty plastic boxes which he would use as seats, an old carpet from a lady who was throwing it away just when he was passing by and let it roll up on the kitchen chair, used hangers from the lost-and-found department when Vrye told him to throw those away, books that he would read in the hot sweaty afternoons of the first year and a dollar-store-bought lamp which he kept turned on all the time. A rectangular wooden cafe table on which it looked like dust would never leave and a small green chair with a black, rounded iron leg. One of the employees from the bowling alley will give him his old mattress which was still in a good shape. In the bathroom after he took out the piled tiles, he hung a blue plastic mirror under the square window above the bathtub and left an opened rinsed can on the edge of it for when he was smoking. But mostly Aaron was going home with bottles under his arm or a six-pack of beer hanging from the top of his slim fingers. Ended up using the empty ones as decoration pieces all over the place without wanting it. Still having the top of a red wine bottle in the bathroom, between the space of the sink and shower. Passing out on the sofa, Aaron felt like he heard them sometimes in the night rolling on the floor. Clinking louder as the sun went down. Louder in his dreams.

The next morning, Aaron woke up nestled on the couch at the sound of the banging door. Opening it, in front of him was Vrye and the owner still going on with their conversation. By the time they left Aaron, the time was showing half past two. He had a couple of hours to kill before his first day at the bowling alley. Aaron was walking around the empty room while taking off his shirt. First thing each morning after waking up he was soaking his clothes in the bathroom sink and leaving them there while warming up the water for his tea. He would start cleaning around the place before eating and then going back into the bathroom and taking a quick shower. Aaron was dragging the sofa around after him when cleaning the high windows with the soaked T-shirt. The light coming inside has changed after. The grey sunlight turned to a warm golden yellow. The chamomile tea would cool by the time he was drinking it and sitting calmly at the table enjoying his burned toast.

Soon after, he cleaned the wooden dining table and chair, feeling his skin gluing to them.

Aaron put on the pair of jeans he had and a blue T-shirt. He was going to walk around before work. Out of habit, he forgot to lock the door but he wouldn't realize it until returning in the night. His straight shoulders were warmed up by the sun when walking down the streets. One could hear his rhythmic whistle before seeing him, walking with his hands in his pockets. Aaron's eyes shining in the golden sunlight from above him. He got to see a park not far from his apartment, the store from the corner of his street, children fighting over a ball in a closed street with only a few cars parked and two women talking on the edge of the road. Two bars, an Irish one and the one he met with Vrye the night before. Aaron lit his smoke while a dentist office was moving to a new location and a young employee was taking out some garbage bags. Loud music coming from a red truck waiting in the intersection for the green light. He arrived in front of the bowling alley one hour earlier and decided to go inside, meet with Vrye, and have a talk with him.

Long shiny wooden floors were shaking at the loud beats of heavy rolling balls. Strong lights above them and switching screens. Aaron's steps were covered by the cheering screams of others. Nodded to the guy sitting behind the counter which waved back at him. Aaron walked to the back where he saw Vrye unplugging an old Donkey Kong machine; had to replace it with the new one he ordered the next day.

He took his time on everything he was doing. He wanted to make the space sparkle. He swept the floor carefully, going around every corner, under each table, and under each machine. He felt like having a smoke but told himself that he will go after he will finish mopping. After, he told himself that he will go after he wiped every table. Aaron wiped them twice just to make sure, just until he was able to almost see his reflection in them. Placed the square red chairs back uniformly at the same distance. Went back in the arcade space and cleaned the screens of the colorful noisy machines which looked like they had never been cleaned before. Shook one of the machines for the stuck coins to fall and put those behind the counter. The sticky dragged fingerprints, which seemed to be from mustard and buttery popcorn, all over them disappeared when Aaron went with the soaked rag over them. With the music and the vacuum on Vrye's footsteps got nearer. His look falling over the whole place while getting closer. Nodding while passing the tables.

'Never saw anyone clean that before,' Vrye said.

Aaron jumped on his feet when hearing him.

'I didn't hear you coming.' Aaron pressed the rag close to his chest leaving a soaked mark on his T-shirt.

'Sorry for that.' He took the remote and turned off the annoying music which was repeating five times a day. 'Place looks great. Can tell you worked hard over there, at your farm.'

Aaron stayed still in front of him after switching off the vacuum cleaner. Waiting for Vrye to finish talking so he could go back cleaning.

'Why don't you finish that one and we go for a drink?'

Aaron turned and looked in the back where he only had the chance to swipe before.

‘I still have to finish that part,’ he pointed, holding the rag.

Vrye laughed. ‘You did more than enough for today. There’s another day tomorrow. And it’s Friday. I’ll say keep your energy for the next two days. Come on let’s go, want to close the place down.’

Vrye looked the doors and Aaron finally lit up his long-awaited cigarette after throwing away the garbage bags. It was a hot night. Walking away from the street intersection, the noise of passing cars slowly disappeared and the two were able to talk quietly.

‘Had the last guy working here.’ He stopped and disapproved with his head. ‘Wouldn’t even sweep before mopping. I was coming for some papers and I saw him with the soaked mop pushing some popcorn under some tables. Then they ask why I always go back and check on everything. Well, that’s why. These guys can’t even do a simple job.’

Aaron took out his pack and held it out for Vrye; seemed like he needed one.

Vrye forgot all about his employees by the time they got there. Aaron had a good time in his company and laughed for a big portion of the night. Vrye chose the drinks for them and offered to pay. Without the nostalgic absinthe glass under his chin, Aaron wasn’t distracted and got to pay attention to Vrye. They became good friends over the next few nights and sometimes Vrye would even help clean out the place so that they could go out for a drink faster.

‘I can see why the old man liked you,’ Vrye said remembering one night the phone call he received.

It was a Tuesday night when he put his trust into Aaron and gave him a pair of keys telling him to close the place down. He left right away after, saying that he had a bad headache.

On the way home, Aaron stopped at the bar but sat at the counter, ending up talking with the bartender, him being the only one there.

As the first night when he arrived, he asked for a glass of absinthe. He once again put the glass close to his chin. Stared at it for another 22 minutes before the bar closed. Without Vrye this time close to him, he drank the glass slowly. Enjoyed the smell of the lost childhood, seeing himself before his eyes running between the hall of his bedroom until the kitchen and back. Wearing his PJs while Father was fixing dinner and soon, he would always have a bottle of absinthe in the apartment.

* *

The warmth of just dried clothes gently touched his skin that morning. His long fingers folded the rest of them carefully and left them on the edge of his mattress. The smell of cheap red wine was filling the closed room. Aaron opened the window wide and poured himself another drink using the same dirty glass from the night before. He dragged the black backpack and put the folded clothes inside, leaving his green sneakers on top of it. Aaron wiped the bathroom counter, cleaned the inside of the fridge with a soapy rag and swept the whole apartment. The sound of passing cars from outside seemed far away, covered by the static of the neighbor's TV channel. He cleaned the dust collected at the corners of the window frames, walked into the bathroom and with the same soapy rag he used to clean the fridge, he slowly wiped the bathtub curtain. Holding it with his other hand on the opposite side while the warm drops were falling at his feet. The time was passing slowly for him that day and he opened another bottle to help it move. He went and swiped the place one more time, washed the window, dragging an old newspaper over it, changed the sheets and put the mattress back in its place. Opposite the brown sofa. Coming in from between the million green leaves covering the barely seen branches, the hot wind from outside. Aaron's eyes were constantly falling on the ready-to-go backpack with the dried muddy sneakers on top of it, which he did not wash since he left the farm. He couldn't help himself but to stop, holding tightly the neck of the bottle. His breath was slowing and if he would watch closely, he could bet he will see and probably find at least one tiny rock from Mr. Jackson's path. Aaron's heart was warming up quickly at the thought of him walking on the path again. From the drawer, he went and took out the money he earned over the year and put them carefully in the hidden pocket from inside his backpack. Sat near it on the mattress; the ticking sound of the clock was louder and louder as the sweat was covering his palms.

He jumped into his black shoes and closed the bottoms of the shirt while stepping outside. The wind wasn't dry outside and he lit a cigarette. Walking down the sidewalk with both hands in the blue uniform pants and whistling between the barely opened lips with the smoke in his mouth. He was seeing himself triumphantly going back in a few hours with a large bag under his arm and feeling the heavy wallet in his pocket. Mr. Jackson walking back and forth as always on the path and start laughing hard when seeing him. Holding out his arms, sometimes slowing down to put one hand to his back and then continue running. His warm breath against Aaron's shoulder when embracing him. He was going home. Both resting on the porch of the cabin in the hot summer night with a cold glass. Out of nowhere, a child almost run over Aaron. With long black curly hair which was partially covering her face cut his way. She hurried to apologize and turned her orange bike to go past the road. Her green jumpsuit was moving fast and got out of his sight between the parked cars. The two side helpful wheels attached to her bike moving faster again. He shook his head and turned the corner into the bowling alley front parking lot.

Aaron went to the toilet to wash the salty sweat off his forehead. He went and stayed propped on a column. Watched the Thursday guys finish the last round of their game. In his sight, he caught Vrye. Back turned. His shoulders were bending over, almost touching his numb knees lifted up because of the red chair. The back of his neck stretched out. His smooth hand covering half his mouth. Aaron walked to him but before getting there, his legs got heavier. His heart was pounding. Aaron took his hand and squeezed Vrye's arm hard as he could to catch his attention. His face turned white in the strong lighting. His shoulders fall heavy at the sound of the loud interrupted speaker of the phone which was sliding out of his stiff hand. Vrye's eyes lost its color along with the red in his cheeks. Eyeballs fixed and empty. Aaron could have sworn that he saw some of his moist dark hair going grey close to its roots.

The untold tragedy. He knew before he told him. The old man was gone. He will no longer wait on the shore for one to go visit him. No one will rush, jumping from the porch chair to go pick up the ringing mobile. His hat was uncovering his neck and ears and he could no longer help himself in dragging it down.

'Something's wrong.'

'It is.' His lips were dried. He gradually raised his head to look into Aaron's eyes but tears were racing down his face before he had the chance of doing so.

The silence broke because of the powerful sobbing and Vrye handed over the phone he was strongly holding; Aaron took it.

His long look at the wooden floor was fading while his sight was blurring with warm tears.

'When is the funeral?' Aaron spoke finally after everyone had left the place and they were the only ones left.

'I'll have to make a couple of calls. Check everything,' Vrye sighed. Lay back in the chair, looking towards his touching knees. 'Will you be there? I think he would have liked that.'

'I don't think…' Aaron struggled. 'I'd love to remember him how I last saw him. Smoking his cigarette on the shore.'

Vrye looked over at Aaron and nodded. 'I understand. I will need you to stay here for a while. Take care of the place for me, would you?' Aaron was afraid of the question. 'You're the only guy I trust, Aaron. For a while, until I work things out for the funeral.'

Mr. Jackson lost his way on the path in Aaron's mind and once again he was walking away from him.

‘For a while, sure,’ Aaron hardly agreed.

‘How do we end up sinning, Aaron?’ Vrye asked preparing to stand. His cracked chin from his childhood shaking.

‘By living.’

Vrye told Aaron not to bother cleaning the place up for the night and that he could also walk home but remembering the untouched backpack from the edge of the mattress he didn’t hurry returning to his place. The excitement he once came in at the bowling alley got sucked up on the column, he was resting on earlier that night.

‘Can’t come yet, old man,’ he whispered and looked at the heavy door at the end of his shift.

He did not have another drink with Vrye after that night nor seen him for another two weeks. When he returned, they only exchanged looks in the big hall and Aaron could feel his sorrow. As he went to talk to him, he knew that there would be no chance for him to go back at the farm, not just yet, and the weeks piled up.

The day was close to an end. The fast-broken clouds on the dark sky were moving faster as nature was more and more silent. Aaron wiped the window glass with the edge of his red shirt hoping for his reflection to disappear. The shift he worked that day was like it never happened and soon he was back in his hollow apartment, standing in one place with his dusty slippery fingers covering his lip and chin. The lamplight was becoming stronger in the corner of the room as the moon was rising higher. The sound of tv channels switching was constantly there. Followed by heavy footsteps from above. The walls were thick and the guy living upstairs did nothing else, or sounded like that, besides pressing the buttons of the remote. Aaron never had one nor wished for it. Back in his old apartment, he had a small old tv which had the cable cut off. He pretended on the lonely nights that he was watching it until falling asleep.

Aaron would constantly wipe the window as much as possible until the reflected figure that was blocking his sight was changing, leaving behind circular marks. He turned around not moving from the spot but forcibly spinning on his toes. Unbuttoning the shirt covered at the end of the shift in dust and sweat. His hands smelling like lemon because of the detergent. The time between those walls was steady. Aaron's shoulders were low and his head was bent behind before realizing he was sitting in the brown sofa. His legs thrown before him which he would move sometimes to avoid the numbness. The changed sheets of the bed were not touched by him for another two days, just until he was able to go move the backpack and the sneakers. Without him and Vrye going out after his shift, he lost interest in standing over alone at the counter bar.

5

I wasn't feeling the cold, my numb body from the ground was, but I wasn't feeling it. In a moment, the path was echoing the sound of me coughing and vomit was coming out washing and taking once with it the dried-out vomit from before.

The funeral was over. Vrye returned.

The hot nights Aaron would roll over in his mattress were over. The insects buzzing from outside were no longer there. The time passed quickly but he could not remember most of it. By every passing day, the window glasses were becoming dustier because of the wind. More empty bottles at everyday light. The nights were getting longer once with the changing colors of the leaves.

The knocking on the steel door was soft. Aaron slid the door. He was facing Vrye. Black shiny shoes, long coat covering his knees, and suit with a black hat which was falling over his forehead. From his hand, a dull yellow tissue was dangling. He walked inside, walked few steps and stopped.

'How are you?' Vrye asked a few moments after.

Aaron nodded. 'How was… You know.'

Vrye went and sat on the sofa. Took off his hat and put it above his legs. 'I can count on the fingers from one hand how many we were there,' he said, staring at his shiny shoes. Vrye was squeezing the fingers of his left hand. 'He was a lonely man, Aaron. No one should be like that.'

He went and sat next to him on a plastic box. Aaron's shirt was unbuttoned and the dark orange sunset light was brightening his face and pronounced collarbones. In his resting hand, he was playing with one cigarette since Vrye showed up.

'I'm sorry for your loss,' Aaron lightly said.

The ceiling was shortly wrapped by the rising smoke. The sky behind Vrye was darkening, the dark violet was getting darker within the square glasses of the windows.

'I wanted him here. But he wouldn't leave the shore. He loved it there. He loved the morning smell of salty water. So much that he preferred staying there alone,' Vrye continued. 'I saw this house once. First time when I moved here. You know that small greenhouse with wooden blinds two blocks away from the post office? I was dreaming of buying it. I would go around, walking for another 15 minutes just so that I'll pass by that house. In the summertime, the front garden is always filled with lilac flowers. That's how I found the place.' His eyes narrowed. Vrye's lips curved and let go of his fingers. 'I was walking one day and I remember it was this hot dry afternoon, luckily there was a bit of breeze and from around the corner, I felt the smell of them. I arrived in the front and I knew from that moment that I wanted the house,' he said. 'But it was just a dream, Aaron. A foolish one.' He laughed, staring down.

‘Having a dream is the most frustrating thing.’

‘Is it?’ Vrye whispered.

‘It’s eating you alive.’

‘What is yours?’

Aaron’s eyes slipped on the black and white floor tiles but did not answer. His shoulders were pressed down by each smoked cigarette.

‘I’ll have to go away again,’ Vrye said after a while. He stood and headed for the door. ‘We’ll talk more about it on Monday, right?’ Aaron was sitting on the plastic box not facing him.

The metal door slid smoothly and closed. Vrye’s echoed footsteps were getting away on the narrow hall until there was silence. Beside Aaron’s left side, from the corner, the pale lamplight was coming alive once with the streetlights.

Monday evening, Aaron arrived at the bowling alley. His breath smelling like alcohol. The arcade space was loud as always. But only two young boys were playing sharpshooter. Violently pointing the red and blue plastic guns to the screen. Aaron was not hearing them anymore, just in the background. Neon, moving colors were covering Aaron’s still face. For the last weeks, he would sit quietly in his chair and wait for everybody to leave so he could start his night shift job. The whole place would rapidly change from the dizzy loud movements to the peaceful freedom of loneliness where he would hide his alcohol in the thermos so the cameras won’t pick up on what was in there. Vrye came out from his office when the door last closed.

Didn’t take more than 15 minutes to sweep the whole bowling alley; Aaron lately would lean letting his weight on the broom and go like so. Next, he cleaned the red chairs and pick up the leftover food from the arcade space while Vrye was filling up some paperwork at one round table. He stopped wiping the screens of gaming machines. The chairs were left as he found them, two under the table one at the top of the table, some dragged out and left near the wall. He would only push them close to the tables. Vrye wouldn't check on him and told him not to bother because the morning shift from the counter was supposed to place them anyway. He had his spare key and was leaving the place as soon as possible. As did Vrye. Once with Aaron and walk with him just before the corner.

'I'll see you tomorrow.'

'Yeah,' Vrye said turning left. 'Wanted to ask you, would you help me tomorrow morning? Have to sort out some papers in the office before I leave. It's a mess over there,' he said passing the road.

'Sure thing. Call me when you wake up.'

They met the next morning in the corner and left together. The air was cool and the soft fallen leaves were sticking to their shoes. Aaron was wearing his black turtleneck sweater and grey loose jeans, a light black autumn coat, and Vrye was in the clothes he had the night before. They walked through a muddy golden alley with tall cement walls on their left side. The tall trees were showing their slim branches. Above, the clouds were dancing around the weak sun, partly covering it.

'When you leaving?' Aaron asked.

'I already packed. I couldn't sleep last night. Maybe an hour, maybe less. But I checked the plane tickets.'

'Why not take the train? Is cheaper no?'

'Yes, but it takes longer.'

‘Mhm.’

‘You can go when I come back,’ Vrye said.

‘Thank you.’

‘I won’t stay for too long. But we have to talk about it already. Called home last night but they had guests over so it was a short talk. I’ll try later today.’

‘When I go back,’ Vrye looked over at Aaron. ‘I’d like to stay for a week, didn’t see the old man in a long time.’

‘It’s true, eh? What? You’ve been working for me almost since the summer started, haven’t you?’

Aaron agreed.

‘Go. Stay for the week. I owe you.’

The road curved and in front of them was the empty parking lot. The black figures were showing in the glass doors. Their steps covered by the jingle keys from Vrye’s hand.

They were half an hour earlier than the guys from the counter who came one after another; one of them stopped in the front finishing his last two puffs from the smoke and holding a cup of cheap coffee which smelled like too much sugar. The desk was covered with cream- and black-colored folders. Some of which weren’t closing because of the pile of papers and others having only two files or less. With both of them cleaning and organizing, the desk cleaned fast. The shelves covered and the folders and paperwork locked in the drawers. That night Vrye stayed and cleaned the place with Aaron, cleaned the tables and chairs while Aaron was in the arcade space but stayed longer, making phone calls after Aaron left.

The last October days he spent at work. Cleaning, organizing and helping Vrye.

Vrye left on a Friday night, heavy rain pouring down and strong wind. Saturday morning, Aaron threw his jean jacket on and left, shaking his apartment. The sound of his bottle getting empty was haunting his ears. As the sound got stronger, his steps got quicker. It was not long before running into the store and rushing to the shelves with shiny bottles. With the absinthe in the white plastic bag, he headed back to the apartment. From the narrow halls of the warehouse, he could not hear the tv static from above and he lay there for a while. Smoked couple of cigarettes, stepping on each of them, then pushing them aside. Between the dark dull yellow walls, he finished the last drop from the bottle and stepped inside, rolling it with his leg and the bottle stopped under the wooden closet.

The room was tall and empty. It was like always dark in there. Aaron was coming back with a couple of bottles and all would go in vain. Mostly laid back on his uncovered mattress and stay still for hours. Raising his head just to take a sip from the cans which he would never let go. With the door always opened, his paranoia grew bigger. But he was not his father. The filth, the smell, and the taste of liquor were getting him back and closer to him. But he was not him, and not would he become.

That morning, Aaron kept his eyes closed, searched with his hand on the floor for his cigarette pack and then the blue lighter. Opened one eye when lighting up his smoke. The sun was up above his head. The strong pale light blinding him. He lay there facing the ceiling, hearing the sound of each puff taken from the cigarette. On the black and white square floor tiles was a forgotten honey spoon, picking up the dust and fallen hair. One bag of clean clothes close to the heater, a rolled pair of socks near the corner lamp, one white sheet covering the left side window waving slowly and rusty movements from the piles above. Let go of the pillow under his armpit. Looking back at his mattress, his upper body was printed in it because of the sweat. Aaron was drinking the last drop from the bottle while walking gently across the room. Making his way to the bathroom to fill up the bottle and take the last drop of alcohol out of it.

From the brown armchair, he was staring over to his right at the round coffee table where the astray poured over and hid under the ash and cigarette butts.

Aaron was sometimes humming the familiar guitar chords he remembers playing in the background from a white and blue radio put on a table behind while falling off his bicycle. The fresh grounded pepper grains running up his nose when father was sewing the pair of red shorts he ripped apart. The cold blue alcohol that makes any child jump and bite their tongue when the first drop touched the wound. His tiny sweaty feet left on the wooden floor when looking out the window raised on his toes and holding the wall. The memories running in his mind over and over.

But they were close. Aaron grew to walk like him, held his head the same way when eating, and resting his arm when he forgets about the cigarette he is holding and it's smoking by itself. They shared a bad habit of leaving pills left wherever, flies resting over them. Seen shadows late at night, hiding deeper into the corners. Swallowed by the lamplight. The last drops of finished bottles gathered at the bottom.

I don't know when. When he became one with the filth. The dirty mattress that got sticky from all the liquids spilled over it got him in the end. Sometimes poking with his slim fingers the holes from it and the bad sewed edges to take out the sponge from inside. Often holding it for the entire night then throwing it away on the cold floor. Looking carefully in the night how it would gently fall down. The smell of mold walls was deep inside his lungs and became for Aaron the welcoming smell of coming home. He grew to hate and fall in love with the room. The quiet that came with it. He lost the notion of time.

It was an easy winter they had that year. There was no storm nor heavy snowing. The alleys were uniformly covered with a white sheet and between the still branches of the trees, snow was falling calmly. The walls were cold to touch but Aaron was moving the square heater after him, leaving it mostly between the mattress and the brown armchair. It was only on one night when the strong wind took the last few layers of snow and blew it all over. Where one could have not walked outside. The tall streetlights turned off once with the whole street. The heavy clouds above moving faster. Before he knew it, the power was back. The road behind the frozen window was sparkling once again with golden, small points of green and red lights.

Wasn't snowing on Christmas morning but it was not melting either. Aaron walked around from 11 a.m. He first entered a small local restaurant with blue walls and colorful foam over its windows. He went and sat near the wall, under some hanged black and white pictures. The two-person tables covered by an un-ironed white tablecloth, a round vase with red plastic flowers in the center, silver cutlery above a folded napkin, and a round glass plate on its right. Aaron's coffee was bitter, without sugar, and he drank it slowly listening to the music. The sweet smell of gingerbread, roasted nuts and marshmallows melting into the hot chocolate was in the air.

Drank the last drop, holding the coffee cup in both hands. It was still warm against his fingers, curving in his covered palms. Put the long coat on and left. The walk was long. The boot prints in the fresh snow were following his every step. Aaron's dark hair was turning white because of the falling snow. The smoke he had in his hand was covering in small watery spots here and there when he would raise it to his mouth. Arriving on his street, he made a turn to the left and decided to go into the park. The bench was sunk under the snow. The bushes were square blocks of ice and the trees around turned white. Aaron put his arm over the bench and with a strong movement, he wiped off half the snow off it. The other half got over his arm and he shook it off after. He fixed his sweater's neck, covering his mouth with it. His legs constantly beating until the brown frozen ground from beneath showed up. His slightly red hands were fighting to open up the bottle. He bent his knees until they were touching each other. Soon he would not feel the cold anymore. His cut gloves were sticking to the cold bottle when drinking from it. He turned his sight and there it was. A white rose with its flowers closed raising up below the fragile snow. He uncovered it when throwing down the snow from the bench. Its leaves were pointy and steady. No thorns. Snow was slowly falling from the branches above. Gently touching the petals of one middle flower. Opening up slowly.

As a child, I was always the tiniest of them all. I remember this Christmas party we had in middle school where I was dressed as an elf and had to stay in the first row so I would be seen. I was looking into Mr. Jackson's big eyes and I was staying straight up reciting my poem with a big smile covering my face. It seemed to me that the lights were falling over his face, over the thin grey hair of his. Holding tightly the brown hat over his legs. I was bending over and over again to pull up the striped socks which were sliding slowly. He couldn't help himself but smile at me. I couldn't tell if I blushed or not but I could feel my check warming. From all the applause at the end, Mr. Jackson was the loudest. His heavy warm hands going on and on. Aaron shook his head as if trying to erase the memory. The night was falling; he then looked back at the rose which was still shining.

Aaron's clumsy steps stopped across the street in front of a duplex. Inside he saw an old lady resting on her chair, watching television. The cream-colored walls seemed warm inside. She was covered by a green blanket and a blue long-sleeved blouse with a pink curved collar. A purple phone next to her on a tall round wooden stand which rang. Aaron could almost hear her happy screaming. Took the phone and rushed in front of the large glass down the living room, where a car just parked. The children from the back seat were the first to jump outside. Aaron left, taking another sip from the bottle. Swallowed it followed by the running feet behind him.

At the warehouse, the floor was dark. The time was showing 7:31 p.m. when he got inside. Turned the heater and kept the coat on. Lit up two red candles then closed his eyes. Aaron covered his face with two big pillows so that he would see nothing on his left nor right. Stayed laying on his back and for a moment there, he was not afraid anymore of what was or wasn't moving around him. Opened his eyes and on the ceiling, circling the light was a small fat worm sliding slowly around it. Jumped up to take another sip. The faces from the wall were not screaming at him no more.

6

Aaron couldn't sleep the night before. He fell asleep for a few minutes and woke at the sound of bread slices that he forgot in the toaster and filled the whole place with smoke. The cold was coming inside after he opened the windows and woke him up entirely. He didn't go back to sleep but pour another glass with absinthe. The bottles were empty and he left them opened in the sink. Aaron was dizzy and dropped some ice cubes on the floor. Later that day, he stepped in the melted water but did not change his sock. Aaron was late for work already but couldn't stand up straight. Raised the warmed bottleneck to drink more and went to get dressed. From beside the armchair, he saw the green absinthe bottle which he shakingly focused to pour in his unwashed thermos. His foot hardly got inside his boot because of the soaked sock. He smashed the sliding door behind him, resting on it for a moment. He left the building. He'll get up from the cold ground the next morning.

Aaron's numb half-opened eye was facing the reflection of a traffic light which somewhere before dawn stopped switching and remained yellow. Two papers of five bucks were taken away by the wind, passing him. His cigarette broke under him, curving around his fingers which were stuck under his heavy body. After he rushed out the bowling alley, a few minutes later he was laying on the cold sidewalk tasting the vomit inside his mouth. His headache got worse with the neon lights and noise from inside. He ran to the counter but forgot to ask for the glass of water. His legs were heavier and heavier and he needed to sit. But if he did so, the whole place would spin. And spin and move and turn around and he needed fresh air. Aaron was swallowing it as hard as he could, not letting it out. The bitter taste was stuck in his throat. It was coming up. Felt it on the back of his tongue. The awful taste. He spits. It was draining down his bottom lip and chin. Took out a smoke and hurried behind the building, scratching his right hand on the sprue wall. Didn't make it.

The first skin layer of his left cheek and from the top of his nose was now getting stuck to the ground. His upper lip smashed and his face was floating in a light combination of vomit and blood.

There were a couple of deposit storages behind the bowling alley with a large unlit and humid path between. The strong white headlights from a parked car were blinding him, he remembered when the door slammed by his back and he tried taking a smoke out of the packet. Contoured cheekbones in the pale moonlight. The trees seemed lonely in the chilly weather. The large street was still awake. At the intersection, the colors were changing. It was red, it was yellow, it was green. His right hand stuck under his body has gone numb. The surface of the vomit close to his face got as dry as making a cracking sound at touch.

The top branches of the trees were moving but the wind didn't seem unfriendly. From above, his fainted body in the middle of the path had his legs forming this curvy "P". The warm feeling between his legs changed quickly. Not so far was a running out light bulb falling, hanging by some uncovered wires. Making his skin look sickening. With that amount of alcohol, it was just about time until one would start throwing up again. The door, without hearing it, was getting opened and closed by the leaving people. Longer into the night, quieter it became. His left hand holding the broken cigarette was bleeding between the cracks.

He wasn't feeling the cold. In a sudden, the path was echoing the sound of his coughing and vomit was coming out washing and taking once with it the dried-out vomit from before. At 2 in the morning, Aaron was shaking until the vomit ran out.

Between his teeth, a slight amount of discolored liquid was still leaking down his chin. Covering his shoulder. His skin has changed its color and his half-opened eye was facing the reflection of a yellow light, a green light, a red light. By the end of the night, his whole body will be covered in dew.

The Irish bar from the corner of the street was late with its closing and closed 20 minutes after 3 o'clock. Aaron's hair was iced, heavy and close to his head. His breath warm. Sore throat and dry nose. A cold breeze spread his vomit closer to his face. The branches of the trees were loud, smashing into each other, just as someone was chopping with an ax. And then, quiet. A single light was on, few houses away. Inside the place, an old radio was playing the second face of a tape.

The shirt under the striped yellow green sweater which was ripped at the collar and had cigarette burn marks on one sleeve was soaking in Aaron's hot, bad-smelling sweat. The heavy dirt which got under his nails when falling got deep into his skin. His right toes were covered by the frozen, soaked sock. From far, the engine of a truck was approaching. A hushed sound that he did not recognize. It stopped. The same sound he would hear when falling again later when looking to tie his boots. His blue lips were steady. His saliva stopped leaking.

The truck tires were sliding smoothly on the path; the driver put it in reverse and begin backing up.

Beep. Beep…

The sound was hurting his ears. From down the road, a pair of black snake model hells were rushing. Getting closer to Aaron. His whole body ached, the pain in his muscle was growing as he became conscious of the repeating sound.

Far, as it seemed like, the shiny small green stone from the medallion was flickering in his numb hand. As it seemed like.

Beep. Beep. Beep.

The reflected traffic light he was unconsciously staring at over the night was covered by the unsteady heels close to his face. The necklace he thought he was holding smoothly turned into the green absinthe bottle.

His runny nose was cleaning the vomit inside it. The sound of waves hitting the shore slowly got replaced by the wind flowing between the branches. His vision was yet blurry, the purple underwear before his eyes slowed down, not sliding to its left and right. A heavy palm hit him on the back of his neck.

'Hey, hey!'

Aaron dragged out his right hand from underneath him and pushed the palm against the ground as if too deep it in the wet sand. He had not had a necklace nor the green bottle in his hands.

'I…' Aaron opened and closed his mouth constantly because of the mud taste he had staying on the top of his tongue.

'Are you all right?' she tried stretching her arm out.

His knee was bleeding when trying to move it. The pain in his toes ran over his body.

'I was…' Aaron was confusingly looking around him, still laying on his elbows with his head falling down. 'The waves.' He stopped and looked down at his feet to check them. 'It was so cold, but,' Aaron tried keeping his eyes open. The burn in them was getting stronger as he would fight it.

She confusedly looked at him. 'I'm sorry, sir, but I don't understand. Need any help?'

'Let him, let him, ma'am!' the driver said, hurrying. 'He needs to get to his senses.'

Aaron lay there without moving while the two of them were sitting closer.

'Excuse me,' Aaron finally replied, 'was there anyone with me?' He fought to say the words, still swallowing the dreadful taste.

'I'm not sure but you were alone when I saw you, sir.'

'Are you sure? You didn't—'

'I'm pretty sure. Were you with somebody?' she interrupted him. 'Was there someone with you?'

'I don't know anymore. The waves, waves, waves.' His voice was fading. 'So close. I could feel 'em.'

The truck driver looked over to her and back to Aaron. He made her a hushed sign with his gloved hand to step further.

With one movement, Aaron was turned, facing them. His elbow slid from underneath him and he was on the ground again.

'A path was there, a path. I think.' Aaron tried getting up. Remembering. His sleeve covered in the gummy leaking vomit spread all over.

She rushed to help him up but stopped when seeing his sleeve.

'I don't. No! I'm fine, I'm fine.' His eyes were shining brightly because of the headlights of the truck but were like no one was in there.

'Look, man, she is just trying to help. I don't know what happened with you but we can't help if you don't talk to us,' he said, fixing his cap over his forehead. 'Ok lady, can you call an ambulance?'

She took off her red soft gloves to search in her purse for her cellphone when Aaron got on his knees, balancing but not falling again.

'Don't. I just. Don't.'

The truck driver was constantly checking him out and reaching his hand to him for whenever he would feel like getting up. Aaron's face swallowed up.

She found the cellphone and hold it in her tiny hand waiting for the truck driver to tell her what to do. He raised his shoulder pointing to Aaron. She didn't put it away but waited.

'There was a path, branches, so many,' he was whispering. Aaron was dropping his eyes as often as he could on his arms. Checking his bruises and scratches. *Where them not from the path?* His palms white as milk, the blue veins were jumping out his hands from the cold. His headache was playing with his vision. He could move his toes now. Not all the way but he would feel them. On his knees, he pressed hardly his body weight upon his palms. The driver got him by his armpits to lift him. She was quiet, her eyeballs crazily moving. Aaron was staying on his feet, holding the arm of the driver which carefully let go.

'He'll be all right?' she asked.

'He'll be fine.' The driver hit him on the shoulders in a friendly manner.

Aaron turned. They both stayed and looked over him as Aaron was limping his way out of there.

Aaron lay down in front of his apartment door. Got his eyes so close to the lock so it would be steady. Fighting his nausea, he grabbed his right hand by the wrist and pushed the silver key in the lock when the steel door slid to the right.

Aaron entered the pink bathroom. The wall in front of him was covered by the large stained mirror. The left top drawers were half opened and hit at the edges as if forcibly closed in a rush. The black empty box from his medicine was somewhere floating in the sink. The big yellow writing from the middle of it seemed shady and wouldn't stop spinning. He looked carefully at himself. Took the comb and push it aside. He then took the bottle from his left and put it in the sink to fill it up with water. Aaron dragged his hand all over the counter searching for his pills. Took over two empty cigarette packs, paused and looked at the naked blond from the ripped magazine, raised the top of a box and put aside the astray. Touched the cigarette with the top of his tongue and spit it out, falling in the water. It was making his nausea come back. Aaron licked the cold mirror in front of him and violently pushed his forehead against it. Gently swinging his head to and fro. His big swollen bug eyes in the reflection were so close to him that Aaron had to step back. Running over a small glass plate covered in ash and round ripped pieces of paper. He was fully dressed; he had the coat on and jumped in the tub with the ice water running. Aaron's chest was pounding stronger and stronger while the tub was noisily filling up with warm water. Took off the coat which fell behind him and started floating in the tub. He moved the bathtub curtains but ended up dragging half of it down. It was dangling, beaten by the heavy water drops. His striped sweater was pushing him down. Aaron kneeled down. Took off the heavy sweater and put it on the floor. Water was running out of it.

The drops were quickly racing down his pale shaking body. Pushed aside with his foot the empty medicine boxes and magazines from the bathroom's floor. Dried himself with a yellow rag that was hanging from the doors lock.

In front of the mirror, he carefully soaped his chin. Bent over the sink and stay as close to the mirror as possible so he could see and not dirty himself. Rinsed his red irritated skin and fixed his hair. Cold drops falling down his chest and shoulders. His short hair was curled around his ears. Cleared the sink; he took everything out and pushed it wherever. Wet everything around. Took the rag he used washing the windows with and dried his face. Aaron turned his head and saw the old lucky coin Mr. Jackson once gave to him.

'I know what I have to do. I KNOW WHAT I HAVE TO DO!' Aaron screamed in the mirror. Salty tears racing down his face. He stood. Walked in the room and checked the empty cans of beers from the glass table. Shook them and listened until one had something inside. Flipped it over and listen to how the beer hit the tiles.

He did not have the strength to pour it all down the drain. The cold air was still hurting his bruised dried face. He was holding the bottom of the bottle so strongly that his fingers got stuck around it. Tears hanging at the corner of his eyes. He was bent over the sink when the smell hit him. The calm familiar smell which was making him sick at his stomach. He needed to sit. He rested each arm on his knees. Shoots his eyes and twisted his wrist so that the alcohol would leak out. The square tiles were quickly covered by the thick green liquid. His wet pants splashed by it. He let his head fall back and he stayed still in his corner. The absinthe was spreading, running underneath him. Aaron could still not let go of the bottle. He delicately stood, leaning against the wall. The smell was everywhere. The mold on the walls was smelling like it, the sheet covering the window, mattress and armchair. His clothes were bathing in it. The humidity coming from the opened bathroom made it worse. He shook his head, trying to make the smell go away. Went back into the toilet and pushed his head above the sink; warm water running down his face.

Aaron took the plastic box he used as a seat. Put in it the empty bottle. Walked around the room and picked every single one; empty or not. The box was full, not having enough space to push the beer cans in too. His feet were sticky over the tiles. While Aaron bent over, picking the last bottle which was rolled under a cabinet, on the ceiling the darkness was cut in half by the first sunlight of the day. The pale light from the cheap lamp decreasing. He got dressed, the warm clothes stopping his shakings. Struggled on the floor to fit his green sneakers on. Aaron grabbed the plastic box, the clicking of the bottles following his pressed steps. The morning sun glowing over them in his sensible eyes. He walked slowly. Anxiously on the iced road. The snow was nearly melted, piled together near the fences. His sneaker covered fast, losing its light washed green color by the deep mud.

Arrived at the path, he put down the box next to the dark wet spot of his discolored vomit. A heavy cry came out and he was fighting it back. The ache in his stomach got stronger and Aaron could feel it tighten. He angrily grabbed the first bottle and smash it to the ground. Pieces and pieces of glass were shining around him. The neck of the bottle didn't break and it was rolling away. The alcohol was draining. Bottle after bottle he would smash with the little force he still had. Echoing the whole path with glasses breaking. From the top of his nose, tears were falling down the ground. Small wet spots rounding him. The smell was driven by the soft wind. The bitter taste of them all was at the back of his tongue. Aaron stepped back quickly but tripped on his clumsy feet. His dried hand was cracked. The warm blood from his palm was covered by the dusty ground. On his back, he searched his pocket for a tissue. He pulled out an old flyer he once took and wiped his palm. A piece of green glass was pointing out his skin. He gently pulled it out and drop it in front of him, seeing it fall. He freed himself. Aaron put on his hood and lay back raising his hands in the air. The shining pieces seemed like moving continuously in his blurry eyes. Slowly, the awful taste was gone. Taking deep breaths. His smoked tongue from all the cigarettes got dryer. His face was covered by his huge smile. His shadow twice its size when standing. Pulled his shoulders back and raised his face to the pale blue sky. He stood over the black plastic box to tie his sneaker. Rested there for a moment and then left all behind. The constant headache was easing and he walked over the million shiny pieces.

Back in his apartment, he couldn't help himself from going and hitting the brown armchair he first saw when entering. For a second there, his stomach stopped hurting and his strength was back. He looked over at the table, at the blue paper taped on the wall, the mattress, broken tiles, clothes all over, the white sheet and he knew he had to get out. Aaron hushed to open the cabinet. There it was. The ready to go backpack he let in darkness for so long. The sneakers playing over the spilled absinthe. Aaron closed all the windows so that the smell won't get out. Threw the backpack over his shoulder holding the coin between his slim fingers. The sliding steel door was wide open behind him. Closed his black long coat on the long narrow hallway.

Letting go of the building door. *I am not like him.*

7

Aaron was playing with the red sweets he knew Mr. Jackson craved for all the time. He was looking down to the bag while waiting in the station. He lit a smoke and waited for the train. Few others were waiting with him, some resting on their luggage and have their wrist around their bags. Aaron lifted his collar to cover his neck and put a pair of sunglasses on. From his left, getting closer, he saw the grey train. It noisily stopped at the station. People were holding their bags, ready to get in. Aaron turned and walked along while finishing his cigarette. He put it out on the back of his sneaker and jumped inside. The train halls were filled with rolling wheels, banging doors and thrown bags. He spotted an empty seat next to the large window. The bag of sweets in his hands warmed up, moving it from one hand to another. The train gradually started moving. The cement pillars from the station, the above screens and cold plastic seats were left behind. The snow was melting. His hands went numb shortly after and his look was fixed outside. On the moving buildings that changed into fields. He was soon out of the city. The narrow halls of the warehouse, the dirty pink bathroom, the broken glass from behind the closed bowling alley. It was all behind. The long fields covered in snow were on both sides of the moving train. The black backpack from between Aaron's legs was steady. He felt the glasses pressing down his nose and he took them off. Drank one bottle of water between the first two stations and melted back in his warmed seat. Waiting.

Almost jumped out of the seat when getting closer and recognized his village. Outside the window was the curved road which meant the train station was close. He went on the left side, standing, holding the steel rail from the hall. The top of the church was raising from between the house roofs. Smoke raising higher and higher from the chimneys. The wooden fences that seemed so far away were deep in snow. The cream-colored walls of the station were covering the view. He saw the red lines near the shop and he knew he was home.

Aaron left the train in a hurry but stopped to look around. Just as he remembered. His heavy steps left the shadow of the station. The evening sky was clear and blue. The fields he waited to see for so long was out his reach yet but didn't lose much time for him to rush in that way. His hair was covering his forehead and running into his eyes as he was passing by on the edge of the road. He was looking for the tall trees from the path but he was not close enough yet. He slowly walked ahead near the road. Passing where he once ran.

The curved road was ending. He could see it. He arrived. Warm tears appeared in his eyes. The path was cleaned with the snow put aside. The leafless trees were taller than he remembered. The wooden fence was curving along with the path, going up. His feet were cold in the sneakers. He did not hurry. Put one step in front of the other, passing the fallen shadows of the trees. Soon, he will find himself stuck in the heavy mud.

The cabin was before his eyes. The windows still covered with the same blue thin curtains. He pressed tighter the bag of red sweats to his chest. Avoided the mud from the front steps and put his hand on the cold handle. Hold his breath before opening the door.

There were always the small things for him. The after-rain smell is driven by a chill breeze while Mr. Jackson was covering his shoulders with an old funny smelling blanket. The slow walks at the rising sun on the path pausing at every few steps and looking above his head at the changing color of the sky in the early sunset. The way he held every single tea bag to his nose and smelled it from beneath his big fingers before putting it in the boiled water from the stove. And of course, there was the way he used to look upon me. His smiling eyes that would light up when Aaron's clumsy steps were approaching. Taking care, until the boy becomes his father.

From across the room, Mr. Jackson was in bed. Covered until the neck with Aaron's old blanket. He got closer, closing the door behind him. The smell hit him. He stopped. Mr. Jackson was facing the ceiling. Hands on his steady chest under the blanket. His mouth was opened just enough to see his front teeth.

Aaron dragged the green chair from under the table and put it closer to the body. The urine smell was not bothering him. He stayed with his clothes on, looking down at the bag of sweets. The writing from above the bag was becoming blurry. Salty tears falling over it. The walls of the cabin were cold, windows froze. The color in his face was gone.

His hands grabbing Mr. Jackson's leg and hold it tightly. Letting his forehead falling over his hands.

'Brought your favorites,' Aaron said between sobbing. The smell was getting stronger and could taste it inside his mouth. He took his hat from his backpack and covered Mr. Jackson's grey head. Aaron opened the bag of sweets and held it close to his face. Mr. Jackson's fingers used to smell like this on the long hot summer nights. He took one sweet and loudly chewed on it. His look lost. Aaron took another one, another and another. Just until he would forget about the smell.

'I was on a vacation. Took me quite a bit to return,' Aaron was talking to Mr. Jackson. Spotting from time-to-time different stains on his clothing. 'The car that picked me up when I left was a red Kia, I found the guy rude but you know, all good at the end. If it wouldn't be, I would have not seen the sea. It was so cold, I can still remember,' Aaron laughed, tears dropping on his lap. 'Hmmm, I see you have a new carpet.' Aaron pointed with the sweet. 'Have you forgotten to clean around here old man?' He leaned forward, embracing his cold hands. Looked carefully then dropped back hitting the back of the chair and continued talking. 'I met this guy one day. He let me work for him.' Aaron choked on the heavy smell. 'You would have hated it.' A smile appeared at the corner of his mouth. 'It was a bowling alley, god damn, it was so loud all the time. Wednesday night was the worst. There were a couple of locals who always used to come. Jeremy and, hmmm, something with an S was the other one. Funny people but they were making way too much noise for their age.' He stopped to catch his breath. 'Actually, if I quite remember you weren't too quiet yourself.' He wiped with the coat sleeve the tear from his cheeks, from the top of his nose and under his chin when it was running down his neck. 'I… I also had a place of my own. It was a pretty good one. I had a fridge, a stove, I bought a sofa chair. I could keep the clothes from lost and found if no one would come looking within 10 days. Some of the clothes were pretty good. I still have them in the box. Remember I wasn't good at folding.' Aaron's voice was shaking at that point. 'I was going to my job, staying there all the shift. Seriously. Had to, right? I was once out and I had a couple of drinks. And then again, the other day. And then I started buying them to have at my place. I don't think I was drinking too much in the beginning. But I don't know. I felt the taste and didn't stop since then. I was often thinking about you, old man.' He was crying out loud. 'I was thinking to come back. But I promised myself that you won't see me like that. But I couldn't stop, so I never came back. And for that I'm sorry.' Aaron let go of the sweet and jumped out from the chair. Turned his back to Mr. Jackson and let the tears fall. He shook his head. Took his time to calm down and wide opened the cabin door. 'But I'm better now. You won't have to see me like that, ever.'

Aaron put on his long black coat from the hanger and started to walk down the path into the city to make the arrangements for the funeral. He walked gently to the path. Stayed in the middle of it and looked at the high branches. 'I'll take care of you, old man.'

The air was cold but not difficult to breathe between the chain-smoked cigarettes. He would focus on the tiny moving match flame that lights up the blue filtered cigarette. Aaron's eyes were shutting down. The things around, the branches, the ground, the pointy rocks, and the thin bushes trunks seemed unreal. Yet, Aaron could lay down with his feet thrown apart on the cold ground. The snow quickly melted under him; his coat covered in mud.

The fields on his right left and in front of him were far and did not look like stopping. The pile of trees was heavily breaking the horizon. He remembered how the old man used to walk the empty path all day long. He never knew nor understood why. But he remembered the stories Mr. Jackson would tell him as a child. All of them were from the path, and how he used to be with his grandmother together. Sharing the last moments on the path before Mr. Jackson saw the last breaths of hers near the path. When her legs lost their strength and she let go. How he ran to her and lean her against the piled dry dirt from the time. Where Mr. Jackson planted the cherry tree.

Aaron shook his head and headed back inside. Took off his coat and searched for a pair of gloves. The cabinet above the sink was empty save for a couple of pain medicine. In the kitchen was nothing but a couple of sponges. Aaron stopped to look back at Mr. Jackson's body. The blanket covering him was moving because of the wind coming in. Aaron took out the clothes from the first two drawers until in the last, back behind he found a pair of red winter gloves. He stopped and wanted to forget the idea. The wind blew the door against the wall. Aaron turned and saw the path again. It seemed crazy, but that is the place where he was the happiest.

I'll take care of you. He put them on the table and went behind the cabin where he found the old shovel. It was nearly broken at the bottom but Aaron fixed it with a nail so it would stay still. He took off his green sneakers, put on another pair of socks and put on a pair of black rubber boots. The coat would have been long and heavy and he dressed up with a dark warm purple sweater. Grabbed the white sheet from the table and covered Mr. Jackson's cold body. On top of the wooden table, Aaron went outside and broke a few dried branches. Tied them up with a string found inside and let them there. The bag of red sweets was above the white steady chest.

Aaron took the shovel which was against the wall. The wood was cold and he remembered the gloves. Put them on and stepped outside. He stopped at the door. Beat the pointed shovel on the floor, easily for a couple of times until he found his strength.

The path was slightly covered by a thin layer of snow which melted. The ground was wet beneath and easy to dig. Aaron got there. He looked back at the opened door of the cabin where he could see the white sheet across the table. Between two trees where the ground was already showing, he fixed the shovel in the ground, held it strongly, put his right foot over and pushed his weight down on it. It went down easily. Took the ground out and threw it on his right. Falling into the snow. Fixed the shovel again, closed the hole he just made. Hold it strongly, leg up, push, going down. Threw it on his right again. The fresh dug soil piled up near him. The smell was printed in his gloves. Deeper into the ground harder it became for him to raise the shovel. He started taking less soil on the shovel to make it easier. His hands begin sliding down on the wooden handle after a while but he did not stop. The sweat was warming up his back. The muscles from his arms and legs were hurting. He had to stop. Lit a smoke, put it between his lips and went on. He had to push harder on the shovel for it to go down, almost jumping on it. The ash was falling down on his rubber boots and freshly dug earth as he got deeper.

The sky would get darker soon. Aaron was almost done. His whole body ached. He put down the shovel at the end and sat down near the hole. It wasn't too deep but it would do. The sun was still above. His hands were numb, took off the gloves and massaged its palms.

He went inside and closed the door. Went through the clothes and changed Mr. Jackson. Cleaned the body with one of the sponges he found, then dressed him in a brown pair of corduroy pants, a blue long-sleeved shirt and black sweater over it. Let the hat cover his head and put his good old leather pair of shoes on. Laid the white sheet on the ground and carefully took the body. His numb hands lifting the stiff body and dragging it in the middle. The dried branches bouquet placed on his chest was pressed down by the tight sheet.

Outside, the orange horizon light was appearing. Aaron was dragging the body, stepped in the mud at the bottom of the stairs but lifted on his knees the body over it so it won't get dirty. In the snow, a heavy mark was staying behind. A large line erasing Aaron's boot marks. Near the hole, Aaron put his feet in the grave and rolled over the body. Got out and looked down. He lit up a candle he found inside at the top of the grave, on the right top.

Aaron was the only one attending the funeral. The white fields getting an orange-like color. He did not have his gloves on. Took the shovel and started throwing the earth back. The heavy hits of ground against the body were filling the long path. The white sheet changing into a dark soaked brown color together with the red running down the shovel handle.

The pile was smaller in the changing weather. The wind was back. His cracked hands were not resting. The bruises from his face turned into a mix of sickening yellow and dark blue with purple spots here and there. From nowhere, he spotted a pale pink petal falling gently down. Laid on the fresh soil. He kneeled, looked closely. More of them were falling. Aaron raised his head. He took a deep breath. His shoulders sank. He forgot about it. His smile curved looking at the cherry tree in front of him. He did not know how he missed it before. It was much taller and stronger than the last time he saw it. The delicate petals were covering the grave of Mr. Jackson.

'It grew big, old man,' Aaron said, holding his tears back. His look was lost above the heavy smelly dirt. He dragged his hand through it. He was back on the path along with Mr. Jackson for the last time. The white of the sheet was still sticking out in one place, before he would cover the last of it. His hand shaking on the shovel. He strongly forced himself up. Caught his breath and continued.

From the far end of the path, the snow was getting disturbed by big footsteps. Aaron was throwing the last layer of earth back on the grave while the wind was spreading the pink petals over it. The sunset from ahead was stretching Aaron's shadow until he was walking over it.

The cracking sound of snow being pressed was getting closer and closer. The footsteps stopped behind Aaron who just finished. With a single movement, he let go of the shovel which fall across the path. The nail holding it steady falling out. The candlelight from the top of the grave was stronger. Aaron raised his hands and covered his tired face. Kneeled, pressing his right palm over the ground. The dirt got under his nail.

From behind he heard movement. He knew it's not from the moving branches nor the cars passing down the far road.

Aaron turned his head. On the long path was standing up straight a dark tall silhouette. He saw the heavy boots at first. He got up. The dirt falling down his hand. The shadows of the trees were mixing with the coming night.

He was looking straight ahead. The black coat was moving behind because of the wind. He took out his hands from the coat pockets and dragged his hat behind. Aaron was breathing heavily at that point. Took a step ahead, and then another. Until the tall man was coming closer once again to him.

'Father?' Aaron said.

CPSIA information can be obtained
at www.ICGtesting.com
Printed in the USA
LVHW051345210921
698347LV00013B/1236

9 781645 756255